THE TEMPLETON MASSACRE

ARROW AND SABER BOOK 4

ROBERT VAUGHAN

WOLFPACK
PUBLISHING
— EST 2013 —

The Templeton Massacre
Arrow and Saber Book IV

Robert Vaughan

Paperback Edition
Copyright © 2018 (as revised) Robert Vaughan

Wolfpack Publishing
6032 Wheat Penny Ave
Las Vegas, NV 89122

wolfpackpublishing.com

Paperback ISBN 978-1-64119-469-3
ISBN 978-1-64119-468-6

Library of Congress Control Number: 2018963969

THE TEMPLETON
MASSACRE

1

Wyoming Territory, November 15, 1878

Lieutenant Colonel Marcus Cavanaugh worked the lever of his Spencer repeating rifle down and back, ejecting a spent .52 caliber round and chambering another. His eyes never left the Sioux savage, who rode off the side of his horse and shot a bow from under the war pony's neck.

The arrow fell five yards short. Cavanaugh adjusted his aim, led the animal by a hair, and fired. The big slug drilled through the war pony's head, killing it instantly.

Cavanaugh levered in a fresh round. He followed the painted body of the Sioux warrior as he leaped from the falling horse and tracked him. Just as he stopped rolling and started to rise from the grass, Cavanaugh fired again. The savage fell, and then lay still.

"Keep firing!" Cavanaugh bellowed at the cavalry men around him. There were twenty city-bred, raw recruits in his party, and some weren't even able to fire their weapons properly. The men scrambled into the patch of brush and trees along the stream.

Twenty Sioux rode away from a sudden barrage of hot lead erupting from the small group of pony soldiers, surprised by the volume of fire. They paused three hundred yards away, riding back and forth as if trying to decide whether to rush the pony soldiers again.

"The rest of you men get off your horses!" First Lieutenant Trevor Powell bellowed. "God dammit, don't you men know anything? Tie your horses and find some protection and get ready to fight again. The hostiles will be back, you can bet your butts on that."

Colonel Cavanaugh looked over at Powell, the only other officer in the detail. At least the man knew what he was doing. Cavanaugh had come into Fort Reno on the Bozeman Trail in northern Wyoming only two days earlier. He was met by Lieutenant Powell, who had come to escort him to Fort Keogh. Twenty fresh recruits were also waiting to be guided to the same post. The fillers for the ranks had been shipped in from Chicago. Fort Keogh was their objective—some sixty miles northwest of Fort Reno on the Westward Trail.

The first day had gone well; they rode thirty miles even with the recruits. Most of them had never seen a horse before, let alone knew how to ride. None of them knew what to do with the two-day ration of hardtack and salt pork they had been issued for the journey.

That morning the Sioux hit them before they were even marching. The same band of about twenty had been sniping at them for six hours now. Three of the young troopers were wounded, none seriously. But the damn Sioux were becoming more bothersome than Cavanaugh could tolerate.

He turned to three recruits he saw standing nearby.

"Down on your bellies, now!" Cavanaugh roared. "That's a good way to get yourselves killed before you even get to your first duty post!"

The Sioux were getting ready for another charge. This time they had formed their war ponies into a phalanx, giving every Sioux warrior a clear shot at his target. They screamed their war cries and charged the thicket where the cavalry soldiers had taken cover.

"Try and hit something this time when you fire those damn Spencers," Lieutenant Powell bellowed at the troops. He squeezed off the first shot, blowing the savage off his war pony.

Cavanaugh fired twice. An enemy horse staggered and went down. He swung his Spencer back and fired again, but the bouncing targets were hard to hit. At fifty yards, the Sioux split in half and charged past the coppice of willow and cottonwood. Not more than a third of the recruits got their Spencer rifles working in that short flurry, which lasted all of a minute and a half.

From the far side of the brush, six Indian horsemen swung back and charged from the other direction. All of the redskins dangled from their mounts on the far side, providing no target save the horse. Half a dozen rifles snarled uselessly. The savages were quickly in range with their bows, shooting arrows into the thicket so rapidly that it appeared as if there were many more attackers.

One of the Indian ponies took a round in the rear quarters and limped away. Its rider was still concealed, except for one bare foot hooked under the top of the surcingle of buffalo hide that fastened around the horse's midsection. The cavalry rifles continued to report, and then the riders were out of range. This time the Sioux rode half a mile downstream, around a bend, and disappeared.

"A casualty report, Lieutenant Powell," Colonel Cavanaugh demanded.

"Yes, sir, Colonel, right away. I'll check the men." The officer jumped up from the grass. He returned two minutes later.

"No new wounds, sir. Just the three minor ones, two from arrows and one rifle shot in the leg."

"Let's ride. I'm tired of this cat and mouse game. This time we'll set up something for them to think about."

The trail left the river and struck out northwest toward Fort Keogh. Less than a mile ahead, a quarter of a mile from the main trail, Lieutenant Colonel Cavanaugh saw what he wanted: a patch of woods with a few tall pines, cottonwoods, and lots of brush. He turned the detail off the trail and led them to the woods.

"Lieutenant Powell, I want you and two men to serve as bait for our little trap. Rope a horse and tie it down. Get some blood from one of the wounded men and smear it on one trooper's face and head. Then you and the other trooper will try to help the man, who will appear wounded."

"Lure them into the trap, sir?"

"Hopefully. I want the three of you out there just past the center of that little clearing. The rest of us will be spread out in the brush so we have a good crossfire on the hostiles when they sweep down on you."

"But will they come?"

"Damn right they'll be here. We have too many horses for them not to get excited. These Sioux live and die by the horse. A warrior judges his wealth by how many he owns. By now they know we're not a seasoned force. They'll be back."

For the next hour, Colonel Cavanaugh expertly positioned the recruits. He put half of them on each side of the woods around the meadow, staggering them so their crossfire would not hit the soldiers on the far side.

At the same time, he asked each man if he could use the Spencer carbine he had been issued. Those who couldn't quickly got a lesson how to load, put in a tube of rounds, fire, and work the lever on the bottom of the trigger guard.

An hour and a half later Cavanaugh saw the first

signs of the hostiles. Lieutenant Powell, on bait duty, also sensed they were near. A warrior ran on foot from some brush three hundred yards from the downed trooper and stared at the trio. When he didn't draw fire, he vanished into the woods.

Five minutes later fifteen warriors screamed their war calls and rode hard from the woods toward the three men near the horse.

Lieutenant Powell had used the time to good advantage. With a small shovel from his gear he had dug a shallow hole for the "wounded" man. The other enlisted man lay behind the horse with the lieutenant for more protection.

The Sioux didn't sense a trap until they were committed. They drove hard toward the three men, but well before they reached them, Colonel Cavanaugh bellowed out the command to fire. This time, all the rifles bellowed forth.

The colonel didn't know if the men were aiming better or if there was so much hot lead flying that the Indians couldn't help being hit. Three of the war ponies collapsed in pain and agony. Lieutenant Powell knocked two riders off their ponies. The trooper who played bait lay in the dirt and calmly fired his Spencer with well-aimed shots.

One Sioux warrior broke away from the pack and headed directly for the woods. The young recruit changed his sights, led the Indian's horse, and killed him with one shot. Lieutenant Powell called out to him.

"Good shooting, trooper."

"Fair. I led him a bit too much, so my shot was two, three inches off."

"What's your name, soldier?"

"Quint Scott, sir."

"You didn't learn to shoot that way in Chicago."

"No, sir. I'm off a farm downstate a ways. Had to shoot for supper usually. If I didn't plug a squirrel or pheasant, I didn't get to eat that evening."

The Sioux seemed trapped. The withering crossfire cut into them. They turned and charged to safety before they were thirty yards from the bait.

Except for one. Unscathed, he saw where most of the fire came from. He ducked low over the neck of his horse and charged for the woods, waving his rifle. More than a dozen shots came close to him, but none hit flesh.

Colonel Cavanaugh jumped out from behind a size-able cottonwood and fired at the charging Sioux. His round hit the warrior in the shoulder. It spun him half around but didn't unseat him. The warrior galloped forward courageously.

"Idiot!" Cavanaugh muttered to himself. The officer brought up his 1873 Colt .45 pistol. He stood sideways as if he were in a duel and fired once at the charging figure clinging to the neck of his war pony. The bullet barely missed its mark.

By then the warrior was within twenty feet of the colonel. His arm stretched back as he prepared to throw a hatchet.

Colonel Cavanaugh waited until the warrior's arm began to move forward. Then he fired. The .45 caliber slug hit the Sioux in the forehead and drove him from the back of his war pony. He died before he hit the ground.

Lieutenant Powell ran up from where he had been waiting. He stared at the body of the Sioux, who had fallen only a dozen feet from the colonel.

"Are you all right, sir?" Powell asked, somewhat incredulous at his commanding officer's close call. Colonel Cavanaugh lowered his pistol.

"Yes, Powell, I'm fine. I'd feel a hell of a lot better, though, if the army taught these men how to shoot and ride before they sent them into situations where they face hostiles."

"I agree, sir. I'll have a little chat with General Sheridan about that."

Cavanaugh smiled at Powell's joke. "You did a good job in the trap, Lieutenant Powell. Remind me to use you as Sioux bait again someday. Now let's get cleaned up and on our way. We should be able to make another ten miles before dark."

They did make ten miles, twelve in fact, before Colonel Cavanaugh pulled them into some trees beside a small creek for the night. Most of the men's two-day ration of food was gone. The detail should have already arrived at the fort, but the Sioux harassment had brought them up Fifteen miles short.

Lieutenant Powell spoke briefly to trooper Quint Scott. The lean farm boy took his Spencer and vanished downstream. Half an hour later the lanky farm boy came back with three big jack rabbits.

The men cleaned and roasted the meat over their small fires, each one bragging about how well he had shot during the battle with the Sioux.

The colonel turned down his portion of the rabbit. He'd been eating too well lately in garrison life and could stand to slim down a little. He spread out his blankets and watched the blaze.

Lieutenant Powell finished, then threw the bones into the campfire. He turned to Cavanaugh.

"Sir, I think I should warn you—you're not going to be welcomed with open arms at Fort Keogh." "That is often the case, Powell. What's the underlying problem at Keogh?"

"The facility used to be called Fort Templeton, as you may know. It was built by Major Sawyer Templeton, and he's been left in charge. It's his own little kingdom."

"So some of the officers resent me because I'm outranking their commander?"

"Yes, sir. That's the mood. Major Templeton will be the toughest to deal with. He's bitter, and told me once he thought of resigning. Then when the papers came through and he saw that you were younger than he is, he really blew up."

"I can imagine. I wasn't always a Lieutenant Colonel, Powell."

"Sir, that's another question I had. It took me five years to get my first promotion. The army is small now

—down drastically after the Civil War from two million men to twenty-five thousand. How in the world did you get promoted so quickly?"

"Luck. I was in the right place at the right time, and General Sheridan took me under his wing."

"No disrespect, sir, but these days in the army, it takes most men twenty years to get to your rank." "That's a fair statement and a question, Powell. I was in a sensitive situation where only I could do the job, and Phil Sheridan got my rank rammed through Congress. He has some powerful friends in Washington." Cavanaugh grinned. "Of course the army being what it is, I could be a shavetail again in a week." "I'll never believe that, sir. I've never seen anyone stand up to a charging hostile like you did back there."

Cavanaugh shrugged. "It was simply the best strategy for the situation. Run away from a man on a horse and you're an easy kill. Stand and wait, hold your fire for a killing shot, and it unnerves the enemy."

They watched the fire for a minute. Cavanaugh had wondered about Templeton. He'd heard that there could be problems. He knew all about the man building the fort and naming it after himself. He was as ready for it as he could be. He figured that Powell would be on his side now. The young soldier had done well, and was favorably inclined toward his new commanding officer.

"Who else among the officers will be antagonistic toward me, Powell? If you can tell me without violating any confidences."

"No trouble there, sir. The next troublemaker is going to be Captain Whipple. He was second-in-command of the fort and figured he'd be in line for an oak leaf when Templeton made Lieutenant Colonel in his job as commander. This man can get downright nasty."

"We have ten officers on post?"

"Yes, sir. You'll make eleven. That's about a third of the number we should have. You know about the strength problem in this army."

"I hope we can get it up to fifty percent. For the time being we'll have to double up and make do." "Yes, sir, the army way."

"Lieutenant Powell, do you know a Sergeant Mike Flynn who was recently transferred to the post?" "Yes, indeed. Most of the men know about Mike Flynn. He came in with six chevrons on his sleeve. First day on post he reported to the Commanding Officer. Major Templeton saw on his transfer papers that he was posted to this garrison under your direction."

"So Templeton ripped off his stripes?"

"No, sir, he just told Flynn to take them off within the next hour. He put him back to private and assigned him to mucking out the stables. You know how precarious an enlisted man's stripes are in a transfer."

"At the pleasure of the facility's commanding officer, the manual reads. Some day an enlisted man's rank will be permanent no matter where he's transferred, just like an officer. At least this time I'll be able to remedy the situation. Who is the Sergeant Major?"

"Another Irishman by the name of McAnuff. Sergeant Douglas McAnuff."

"He earned the stripes? Is he a good man?"

"Far as I know. As I recall he's been at Fort Templeton—sorry, at Fort Keogh from the time the army started the building."

"With Templeton?"

"Yes, sir."

"Well, I'll find a spot for him."

They sat a moment watching the sticks burn down to coals and white ash. Cavanaugh loved to watch a wood fire burn.

"Are you happy in the army, Powell?"

"Yes, sir, Colonel."

"Did you go to the Point?"

"I did, class of Seventy-two. I've been in the army for six years."

"Good, Powell. I'm glad to have you in my command. Anything else I need to know about the fort or the people?"

"We're short on enlisted men and on horses. Our supplies come through in fairly good shape, but we don't have any ammunition for target practice. If those men today could all shoot as well as the lad from downstate Illinois, we'd have put down half those Sioux."

"I agree with you. I'll see that we get at least twenty thousand rounds for target practice. General Sheridan is convinced that units in hostile situations should have target practice for every man on post."

"Even the officers, sir?"

"Especially the officers. I noticed that you do all right with a Spencer."

"Thank you, sir. I spend some of my wages to buy rounds for practice."

"You won't have to do that anymore."

Colonel Cavanaugh liked the young officer. He was five-feet, eight-inches tall and maybe 140 pounds wet. He had brown hair, green eyes, and was cleanshaven. He seemed to be good with the men—even the raw, untrained recruits. Powell would be a good man to rely upon.

"What's your position in the fort, Powell?"

"I'm commander of G Company, sir. None of our units have more than one officer."

"That's what I've heard. They tell me this is a palisaded fort, one of the few that the army has built in the last fifty years or so. Is there that much of an Indian threat here?"

"Yes, sir. We send out wood details to cut logs to bring back to the fort for firewood. In the coming winter we'll be out there every two or three days. The wood details are one of the Sioux's favorite spots to hit us."

"But that must be within three or four miles of the fort?"

"Yes, sir, two miles at one place, but we're moving out a little now. We'll start wood details soon so we can get a good supply ahead. We're supposed to keep a two months' supply, but that's hard when it really gets cold."

Cavanaugh smiled at the young officer across the fire. He was going to have a good career if nobody ruined him or drove him out of the army.

"About time for me to turn in, Powell. Have the troops up at five-thirty, as usual, and we'll get into motion by six."

"Yes, sir, Colonel. They'll be ready."

2

THE DETAIL MOVED OUT PROMPTLY AT 6:00 A.M. THERE had been little for breakfast, but Marcus Cavanaugh promised the men food shortly after their arrival at Fort Keogh.

As they rode, the colonel thought about the testimony he had recently given at yet another congressional hearing on General Custer's Battle of the Little Bighorn. It seemed that the clamor over the tragedy would never go away. He had talked for three days in front of a house subcommittee, informing the congressmen of everything he knew about the men involved, and why he thought the tragedy occurred.

He had been in Washington, D.C. for over a month, preparing for the hearings and testifying. During that time, he had long discussions with the Secretary of War, and others in his department.

General Sheridan was in town for a while, and they reminisced about their days in the field together.

By the time the general left the Capital, Sheridan had convinced the War Department that Cavanaugh should be promoted to colonel. General Sheridan claimed he had a specific and consuming need for an officer at that rank, and that no other man in the Military Division of the Missouri was available or qualified.

Much to General Sheridan's surprise, the War Department agreed. They submitted the recommendation to Congress, which passed a special bill two days after Marcus Cavanaugh had charmed the subcommittee by demonstrating his knowledge and his dedication to the U.S. Army.

Marcus was grateful, and he had taken his new assignment from General Sheridan with eagerness. Unfortunately, it was getting off to a miserable start.

There seemed to be few travelers on the Westward Trail as it worked its way up toward Montana. Indian problems had magnified. The riders came across a dry stretch, and Cavanaugh gave the command to let the horses drink at the next body of water.

"How much farther, Lieutenant?" he asked Powell.

"About five miles, sir. We've been riding along the edge of the Bighorn mountains for the past ten miles. We passed Clear Creek about five miles back, so we're getting close."

"Do you come here for your woodcutting, Powell?"

"No, sir. We go in the other direction, up Little Sandy Creek north and west. It's the closest woodcutting area right now."

"How are the wounded?"

"Two of them are fine. The one with the bullet wound is looking a little ragged. We've a good physician at the post who'll take care of him quickly enough."

"What's the general, lay of the land around the fort, Powell?"

"The fort itself is built on a plateau between two branches of Sandy Creek. To the east is a high point we call Pilot Hill. West of that is another ridge we call Sullivant Hills. To the southwest of Sullivant Hills is Lone Pine Ridge. We have pickets and heliographs on both Pilot and Sullivant Hills for early warning of any attack."

A short while later, the troops were within sight of Fort Keogh. Colonel Cavanaugh stared in amazement. He had heard it was a remarkable fort, the best that the army had ever built, with palisades, towers, and fortifications. Lieutenant Powell rode up beside him.

"Sir, the fort itself is six hundred feet by eight hundred feet including a handsome parade ground, securely enclosed with eight-foot-high palisades."

"I'm impressed, Powell. It's the best fort I've ever seen in the army. Let's get inside."

Powell rode ahead to announce the new commander's arrival so there could be some kind of a reception committee. But when Colonel Cavanaugh led his recruits through the main gate a few minutes later, there was only the usual salute of the gate guard. The current fort commander was nowhere in sight.

Colonel Cavanaugh returned Lieutenant Powell's salute.

"Guess I'm your welcome committee, sir."

"Good. Get these recruits put where they belong, then come and give me a quick tour of the fort."

Five minutes later, the two officers walked around the compound. Cavanaugh was even more impressed once inside the fortress. A continuous banquette of heavy pine logs had been set three feet into the ground, dressed on the sides to match, and every fourth one had a flaring loophole cut down a foot from the top of the log. They presented ideal firing positions. At the front corners of the structure there stood enfilading blockhouses with portholes for the Howitzers.

Sturdy buildings of sawed lumber near the main gate served the band, the sutler, and the guard house. Directly in front of them was the parade ground, over four hundred feet across with a flagpole in the center. Across from it stood the officers' quarters, six large buildings; behind them were the administration buildings.

Along the wall to the west of the officers' quarters were four, solid two-story buildings filled with the various companies of enlisted men. A similar row stood at the opposite side of the parade grounds. Behind those quarters was the cavalry yard. Beyond the interior fence stood the teamster quarters, wagon masters and teamster's mess, and the old shops for the mechanics. The stables took up most of the eastern half of the north wall and all of the east side of the fort wall.

Various other shops, non-com and staff buildings, and the A.C.S. and A.Q.M. buildings finished the tour.

Colonel Cavanaugh waved at his escort. "Let's get back to headquarters so I can meet Templeton. I'd like to compliment him on the construction of the finest fort in the army today."

They walked past a battery of cannon lined up on the south side of the parade grounds to the fort commander's office. It was a two-story building made of framed lumber and surmounted by a watch tower that overlooked the southern palisades of the fort.

That was when Cavanaugh noticed the differences in the construction. The officers' and men's quarters were built from logs. The warehouses, which were eighty feet long and twenty-four feet wide, were framed.

They walked to the commander's office. A soldier posted outside brought his rifle up to present arms in a salute. The officers returned it and opened the door.

The inside of the commanding officer's headquarters looked like a dozen others Colonel Cavanaugh had seen. A sergeant's desk, six feet from the door, blocked the path. Beyond that were two doors, the left one for the commander, the right one for his second-in-command. A sergeant major with a heavy moustache looked up from his paperwork.

At once he stood and came to attention. "Yes, sir! Good morning, Colonel. The commander is expecting you."

"At ease, Sergeant. Show us the way."

The sergeant moved around his desk, shot a glance at Lieutenant Powell, and then marched to the left-hand door. He rapped three times, opened the door, and led the two men.

"Major Templeton, sir. Colonel Cavanaugh has arrived."

The man behind the desk rose. His hard brown eyes stared at his replacement for just a moment. Then he came to attention and snapped a precisely correct salute.

"Welcome to Fort Keogh, Colonel Cavanaugh."

Cavanaugh waved the salute aside. He evaluated the man in a few seconds. Templeton was about five-ten and heavily built, 200 to 210 pounds. He had huge hands and mammoth arms. His jaw was square and stubborn. His jet black hair had been cut severely, and he wore a full black beard, closely trimmed. Cavanaugh remembered the man was thirty-eight years old—five years more than Cavanaugh. That would rankle him.

"Thank you, Major Templeton. We had an interesting trip and I've just had a tour of the fort. Major, this is the best laid out, engineered, and constructed army fort I've ever seen. It's easily the finest anywhere in the United States Army. You're to be congratulated."

"Thank you, Colonel." For a moment a spark of pleasure filled the man's rugged face. Then his eyes turned cold again. "Colonel, you must be tired after your long ride. Powell, show the commander to his quarters and then escort him to noon mess. The cook has prepared something special for us today."

"Yes, sir," Powell said. He turned to Colonel Cavanaugh. "Whenever you're ready, Colonel. I'll wait outside." He turned and left the office, silently closing the door behind him.

When the door clicked shut, Templeton dropped into his chair. He looked up with thinly concealed anger. "Colonel, I've moved out of the Fort Commander's quarters. They've been cleaned properly and are ready for you. All of my personal gear is out of this office and you can move in this afternoon. There will be a formal change of command at three if that's satisfactory."

"Yes, that will be fine." Cavanaugh paused. He wanted to snip this anger in first flower if he could. "Templeton, I want you to know that I didn't ask for this assignment. I was ordered here, just as you were." The black eyes looked up with hatred this time.

"Colonel, that doesn't change much, does it? I'm still being demoted."

"No, Major, you were the acting commander here. Your records will reflect that. There has been no criticism of your work. It's a normal re-staffing procedure, long overdue."

"I should have been promoted, and . . He stopped, surprised that he had said such a thing.

"I agree with you, Major Templeton. Somehow the army didn't. I'm sure you'll have your star before you retire. It's my hope that we can have an orderly change of command without any upset or changes in procedures."

"It doesn't matter."

"It matters a great deal to me, Major. You will be my assistant commander, and as such it should matter a great deal to you as well. I also hope that any animosity you have toward me will vanish in a hurry and we can work together."

Templeton stood and saluted. "Whatever you say, sir! I am your errand-boy, sir! Give me all the shitty jobs, sir!" Templeton remained rigidly at attention.

"Sit down, Major Templeton. Your childish tantrum is unworthy of a major in the U.S. Army. I'll forget about this. But from now on I expect to have your unqualified support."

Templeton sagged. He covered his face with his hands.

Colonel Cavanaugh took a long breath and stood up. "Major, I'll see you at noon mess." He turned and walked out of the room, closing the door gently behind him.

Outside the commander's office, Powell jumped to his feet and led the way out the door.

"Lieutenant, I'd like to see those new quarters of mine," Colonel Cavanaugh said.

The fort commander's quarters were adjacent to the headquarters building. They were set up for a family: Since this was to be a secure fort, it was built with the idea that wives and families of officers would live there. Indeed, many women were at the site from the very first phases of construction—in a warzone where they were in danger.

There were three bedrooms upstairs, a spacious dining room that opened into a much larger living room so the two could be used for socials and dances at the whim of the commander or his wife.

The house was furnished, albeit sparsely, but there would be more than enough for a single man. A married officer usually brought some of his own things along.

Cavanaugh poked through the rooms, then came back to the kitchen. It was stocked with supplies. Three troopers stood at attention. Lieutenant Powell came in.

"Colonel, you'll be needing an orderly. These three men have applied for the position."

"Wait in the other room while I talk to these three gentlemen."

Powell left at once. Colonel Cavanaugh sat in a sturdy chair at the kitchen table. All three of the men were corporals, which meant that each had several years in the army. Evidently the policy here was to have a two-striper for the commander's orderly.

"Gentlemen, I'd like your first names please." They told him in order. Colonel Cavanaugh nearly disqualified the second man in line. He was sharp-faced, raw-boned, had a tick under one eye, and was not as neatly turned out in his uniform as the other two.

Their names were Harry, Lloyd, and Felix. He memorized them instantly. "I'll ask a question and you'll answer in order one after the other, do you understand?"

He talked to them for ten minutes, and to his own

surprise picked Lloyd, the man with the tick under his eye and the strange haircut. Lloyd was articulate, sincere, and eager to do the job. When the other two were sent back to their units, Marcus talked with Lloyd and found out he was twenty-two years old. He had been in the army for four years, came from Virginia, and considered himself an excellent cook. He could also use a needle and thread. His last name was Zedicher and his father was English and German.

"Around home Pa was mostly German," Lloyd said.

"Lloyd, I'll be taking most of my meals here. Look over the larder and order what you want from the quartermaster. Have him give me a bill. Every item will be paid for. I'll have my noon meal in the mess to meet the other officers. You're dismissed to go to your quarters and move your gear here. Pick out the room you want to stay in. You'll be living here from now on, and you'll be excused from all other duty." "Yes, sir. And Colonel, thank you. You won't be sorry that you picked me."

Lieutenant Powell stood up as Cavanaugh came into the living room. He was grinning.

"Good choice. Not only did I win a bet, but you picked the best man for the job. Lloyd is a good soldier and a fine cook. Now we should be heading for the mess."

Colonel Cavanaugh allowed himself a small smile. "Lieutenant, today I think even the most hard-to-get-along-with army cook will hold noon mess for me."

. . .

Lieutenant Powell chuckled as they stepped outside. The air was nippy.

"Starting to cool off, sir. We can expect our first snowfall anytime now. It'll soon be time to dig out our overcoats."

A small structure near the fort hospital at the end of the headquarters building had been converted into the mess for those officers without wives. This noon, every officer in the fort would be there to get a look at the new commander.

Cavanaugh knew what to expect. He'd attended more than his share of such gatherings—but always on the inspecting end, never the one under the microscope. The short walk was over. Now he could use all of the command presence that he could muster.

Powell opened the doors and stepped back, letting Colonel Cavanaugh walk into the room first.

"TEN . . . HUT!" one of the officers barked. The nine men in the room stood quickly and came to attention.

"As you were, gentlemen. My name is Marcus Cavanaugh and we're going to be working together on this post. Thank you for coming to this informal get-together. Later on I'll want to have interviews with each of you so I can become better informed and acquainted with my officer corps. Now, what's for dinner?"

The tension broke and they all sat down. The chair at the head of the table was reserved for the new commander. When Cavanaugh sat, he noticed that there was a stemware wine glass filled with a port wine at each place setting.

Lieutenant Powell lifted his glass of wine and stood. "Gentlemen, I propose a toast to our new commanding officer, Colonel Cavanaugh."

They all stood, except Colonel Cavanaugh, and lifted their glasses. "To Colonel Cavanaugh," they said in staggered unison.

"A toast to Fort Keogh," another man said. Colonel Cavanaugh stood for the second toast. There were half a dozen more until the glasses ran dry. For the noon meal they had steak from a freshly-butchered steer, peas and potatoes, fresh baked bread, thickly sliced, and fresh butter from one of the lieutenant's wife's larder. The woman had found a wandering cow near the fort one day, caught it, and tied it up. It probably once belonged to some emigrant family. The lieutenant's wife had been a farm girl, and now was the only one on post to have fresh milk, cream, and, from time to time, real butter.

When the meal was finished, Colonel Cavanaugh knew he was expected to say a few words. He stood and the chatter quieted.

"Gentlemen, it's good to be here. This is the most magnificent, well-engineered, and well-built fort in the United States today. I've told Major Templeton that I think he'll go down in military history as the man who built the ideal fort in hostile Indian territory.

"I've also heard the fort called by several names. The official name for this facility is Fort Keogh.

Perhaps some of you didn't know Captain Myles Keogh. I rode and fought with him for two years. He was one of the finest field officers I've ever known. He had that sixth sense of combat. He knew what to do instinctively. He told me once that if you have to stop and think what to do next when the Sioux or the Cheyenne attack, you're already half dead.

"From now on I want every officer to make sure that this post is referred to only as Fort Keogh. Captain Keogh died with Custer at the Little Bighorn."

He paused and looked at the men.

"So, we're on board, and this group has broken bread together. We'll have the changing of the command ceremony this afternoon at three, Major Templeton tells me. I look forward to working with each of you, and to performing the mission of this fort, which is to guard as best we can and keep open the Westward Trail that goes past our front door. Thank you, gentlemen. Now I have some more settling in to do before three this afternoon—which I might add, includes a good hot bath and a fresh uniform.'"

"Teeeeeen . . . hut!" someone called. Ten chairs scraped back quickly, and the officers jumped to their feet, braced at attention. Lieutenant Colonel Marcus Cavanaugh marched out the mess hall door.

Lieutenant Powell caught up with him on his walk toward the commander's quarters.

"If there's nothing else I can do for you, Colonel, I'd better see to getting my men ready for the parade."

"You're relieved of your special escort duty, Lieutenant Powell. And thanks for the briefing. I'll want your evaluation of each of the other officers, so be thinking about it. Right now you're the only sympathetic ear I have on the post."

Back in his quarters, Colonel Cavanaugh was pleased to find that Lloyd had anticipated his bath. A big copper boiler filled with water was near the boiling point on the kitchen range.

"Lloyd, what do we have for a bathtub?"

"Army's best, sir," Lloyd said with a grin. He pointed to a circular wash tub. "That's the largest one, sir, a thirty incher. Most of them are only twenty-four inches across."

"Outstanding, Lloyd. Do we have any cold water or do I scald myself?"

The corporal had provided three buckets of cold water as well and put them beside the tub. Together they lifted the copper boiler off the stove by its wooden handles and poured the water into the tub.

An hour later, Colonel Cavanaugh paced the big living room. He had put on a fresh uniform that Lloyd had ironed for him: dark-blue officer's coat with shoulder boards, his formal saber and sash, and the ungainly dress helmet in dark blue with the yellow braid and emblem. Its tall yellow tassel made all the officers look like Prussian generals. At least the fancy braid had been taken off the sleeves of officers' dress coats, except for brigadier generals and above. He checked the yellow band down the light blue trousers, then his polished boots with the square toes. He was ready to take command of the fort. He just hoped the fort was ready for him.

Since the parade wasn't due to start until three, Colonel Cavanaugh went over to his office, greeted the sergeant, and asked for the daily report. He studied the troop strength on the post.

Fort Keogh was built to hold a thousand men and officers. Now it had less than a third of that number, even though there were full strength units sitting around doing nothing back at Fort Laramie. It was a matter he'd bring up with General Sheridan. The fort was woefully undermanned for the job it was supposed to be doing. Marcus figured he could squeeze another three hundred men out of the general. That would be a help.

A knock sounded on the door, then it opened. Sergeant Major McAnuff looked in.

"Sir, it's time. The troops are assembling and Lieutenant Powell has a mount for your approval." Lieutenant Colonel Marcus Cavanaugh stood. "Yes, the ceremony." He walked outside for the changing of command.

3

THE COMPANIES WERE DRAWN UP ON THE PARADE ground in a Regimental Front. The officers left their commands and stood next to the reviewing stand, an eight-foot-square platform that rose two feet off the ground. Major Templeton and Colonel Cavanaugh stood stiffly at attention on it. When the officers had gathered, Major Templeton addressed the gathering in his parade-ground voice.

"Gentlemen and troops of Fort Keogh. This day, November sixteen, in the year of eighteen hundred and seventy-eight, I, Major Sawyer Templeton, do release command of this facility, Fort Keogh, and turn over the function of command to Lieutenant Colonel Marcus Cavanaugh. Colonel Cavanaugh, I salute you."

Down the line, the company commanders and sergeants in charge of the formation echoed the call.

Every man on the post saluted the new commander. Colonel Cavanaugh came to the front of the stand and returned the salute. The three hundred men dropped their hands to their sides.

"Officers and troops of Fort Keogh, I'm honored to be here today and to assume command of this post. We will continue to fulfill our mission to protect the westward trails for emigrants and commercial ventures. To mark this day, all duty assignments except those mandatory to the functioning of the post are cancelled for the rest of the day." He turned to Templeton. "Major, let the parade begin."

Major Templeton came to the front of the stand and bellowed out orders. The officers in charge of troops returned to their commands and the soldiers formed into companies four abreast. The fort band led off the parade, and each group was given an "Eyes right!" as the men marched smartly past the reviewing stand, saluting the new commander.

The marching men were followed by a crack show team of twenty-four cavalrymen on nearly matched black horses. The riders were good, and Cavanaugh was not surprised to see Lieutenant Powell commanding them as they pranced past in well-disciplined formation. The men continued around the parade ground and came back into review formation. They were dismissed by Major Templeton.

Colonel Cavanaugh mounted his bay and rode back to his headquarters office. He called in a runner and ordered him to find Private Mike Flynn in the stables.

"Tell him to get cleaned up and report to the commanding officer," the colonel instructed. He went to his door and looked out at the man sitting behind the desk. "Sergeant Major, would you come in for a moment?"

McAnuff stood up and walked into the office. "What can I do for you, Colonel?"

"The first thing you can do, Sergeant, is to be understanding. I had a man transferred to this post, and he was dumped from his rank and sent to the stables. I want you to consider how you would feel if that happened to you."

"I'd be mad as hell."

"I'm sure Sergeant Major Mike Flynn felt the same way. Flynn has been with me at various commands for three years now. He'll be replacing you here as Sergeant Major. You will be transferred in rank to any position now open. Quartermaster would be the most choice spot I would guess. I've sent for Sergeant Major Flynn. I want you to work with him for the next three days, acquainting him with your procedures and the entire operation of your office."

"Sir, I . . ." McAnuff stopped.

"Surely, Sergeant, you've heard of this happening before. You must have known that I transferred Flynn here for this purpose. I can't believe that you didn't know he would be replacing you."

"Yes, sir," McAnuff said, through clenched teeth. "You'll be treated fairly, Sergeant Major, as long as you do your job and maintain discipline. You might be thankful that you are not stripped back to private and placed in the clean up in the stables as Sergeant Major Flynn was."

"Yes, sir," McAnuff said, his face red with anger. "McAnuff, you might remember also that a transfer for you is an option. If I see any lack of cooperation from you in the next three days, or any trouble from you after that, I can guarantee you that you will be a private again and in the stables permanently. Or the stockade or a federal prison after a court martial. The way you finish your army career is strictly in your hands, Sergeant Major." Cavanaugh paused for a moment. "That's all."

McAnuff saluted, stepped back a stride, did a formal about-face, and walked out of the room.

A moment later, there was a knock on the door. A captain came in.

"Captain Whipple, Colonel, now Quartermaster Officer. As the ranking officer on the post next to Major Templeton, it's my honor to inform you about a reception to welcome you tonight in my quarters. There'll be dinner and dancing. The four officers' wives on post have been planning this for two weeks." "That's very kind of them, Captain Whipple, but it's not necessary."

"Oh, but it is, Colonel. You don't know my wife. I'd be skinned alive if she didn't get to have this party. She'd been looking forward to it ever since we learned of your assignment here. She says we'll start the festivities about six, eat at seven, and have dancing until the fiddlers fall asleep."

"Thank you, Whipple. I'll try to be on my best behavior. What's the strength of most of our companies?"

"Out of a normal strength of ninety men we have forty-two on the average in most of our units, sir."
"Does it vary much?"

"No, sir. I'm afraid not. We have casualties almost continually from the hostiles. Patrols are the most costly, but even the wood detail takes casualties on every third sortie. Now and then we get a few replacements, such as the twenty men you brought in."

"Thank you, Captain Whipple. I'll be evaluating our whole mission here and trying to get more replacement troops from General Sheridan. I'll be looking forward to the reception tonight."

Whipple saluted and left.

Colonel Cavanaugh leaned back in his chair. He was relieved to find that a reception had been planned. It was normal procedure, but he thought perhaps Templeton had squashed that as well. Maybe Templeton didn't have as much influence with the other officers as he had first suspected. Tonight would tell. He would have to wait and see, and in the meantime try to steer a neutral course through the white water.

The moment he opened the door to his quarters he smelled something good cooking. Lloyd came out of the kitchen with a large wooden spoon in his hand.

"Colonel, sir, I went to supply and found a new pair of boots in your size. They're polished up brightly for tonight's reception. I also washed and ironed a dress shirt for you. If you take off your dress uniform, I'll see what care I can give it before the party."

"Thanks, Lloyd. The fresh shirt will be enough. Boots? The right size? I have a hard time finding boots I like."

"These are exactly like the ones you're wearing, except not trail worn, sir. Is there anything else I can do for you before supper?"

"No, Lloyd, I'm going to lie down for a minute. I've heard Napoleon took three naps a day. Today, I'll emulate him by a third."

Cavanaugh went into his bedroom, shucked out of his officer's jacket, and hung it over the back of a straight chair. He dropped on the bed and tried to relax. With a little bit of strong punch and a flask or two to loosen the gentlemanly tongues at the upcoming reception, there would be some real emotions leaking out. Perhaps he would hear the resentment he felt. He wanted to be ready for it.

Colonel Cavanaugh knew it was best to be a bit late at the affair to give everyone a chance to arrive. He came into the building that housed the two officer families at exactly twenty minutes after six.

The receiving line was quickly set up, and he met the ten officers on the post again, as well as the four wives. He promptly forgot which woman went with which man except for Linda Templeton. She was a wafer-thin little woman who had left three children in Missouri with her sister. She was going back now that she had no future duties as a commander's wife. Cavanaugh had not been aware Templeton had a wife on the post.

Then the party continued. There was a spread of two kinds of delicious Wisconsin cheese that had been aged for two years. That went with a good port wine that one of the officers had brought as his contribution. Almost at once, Cavanaugh was surrounded by three young officers who were asking for his opinion on a matter.

"It seems to me," Captain Whipple said, "that the whole strategy of the Battle of the Little Bighorn was one mistake from start to finish. There were so many things that Custer and his men did wrong."

Whipple eyed Colonel Cavanaugh, openly throwing the challenge to him for all to see. He smiled innocently. "I understand you had ridden with some of the men who died with Custer, Colonel. What was your evaluation of those men?"

Colonel Cavanaugh took another sip of his wine. "This is a battle that will be argued one way or another for years. No one can be sure who was right and who was wrong. Yes, mistakes were made, but I can't tell you about them in ten minutes. I recently spent three days before a committee of the House of Representatives, giving them my evaluation of the men and the battle. If any of you really want to know, you can see a transcript of my statements in the Congressional Record."

"But you agree that Major Reno made some blunders, and Keogh should have moved his troops faster as the relief force," Whipple said, refusing to let the subject go.

"Gentlemen, the record on Major Reno is easier to read. Yes, mistakes—perhaps errors in judgement— were made in those few hours. But as far as Keogh goes, he was under orders. He carried out those orders as every one of you must do. He was an innocent victim of the mistakes of others."

As the men talked, Major Templeton pushed into the small circle of officers. Templeton was red-eyed already. His uniform was a bit askew, and Cavanaugh figured the man had been drinking whiskey since the parade that afternoon.

"Hell, I don't believe in innocent victims," Templeton said in a bellicose voice. "Every man earns what he gets, good or bad. Hell yes, the men who rode with Custer made mistakes, dozens of them. Just staying in Custer's command was a stupid thing to do. Those officers should have known by that time what a show-off Custer was. He was a man who thought only of promoting himself, getting his name in the papers, and winning back his stars."

Colonel Cavanaugh glowered as the officer completed his little speech. "Captain Keogh was a brave and gifted man. He would have advanced fast and far in the army if it wasn't for his assignment. He was requested by Custer. He obeyed his orders and he rode with Custer right to his death. As long as we're talking about Custer, I rode with the general for almost a year.

I left a month before the Little Bighorn attack to report to Omaha. Does the major mean that I, too, am a stupid man for serving under Colonel Custer?"

Templeton swayed against Captain Whipple, who caught him and eased him erect. Templeton lifted his brows.

"Present company excepted, of course, Colonel Cavanaugh."

"So noted, Major." Cavanaugh stared at the drunken officer for a stony moment, then turned to another group where the conversation was less volatile.

The officers were talking about Indian fighting. Lieutenant Powell was recounting the battle they had coming up the trail from Fort Reno.

"Twenty of them, Sioux I suppose. They kept sniping at us, trailing us, and badgering us. After the last time, Colonel Cavanaugh said we were going to set a trap for the devils."

Powell went on to tell about the trap and how well it worked.

"What I'm saying is that we've got a commander who knows how to Fight the Indians, and has more experience at it than all of us combined, I'd guess." "Then you think the Sioux are good fighters, Powell?" Lieutenant Nate Brown asked. Brown commanded E company, infantry.

"How long have you been on post, Brown?" "Three months."

"Haven't you had a few fights with the Sioux?" "Just

some wood detail skirmishes. Nothing to indicate that they can fight."

"They can fight, Lieutenant. I'll put any fifteen-year-old Sioux against you any day in a one-to-one battle with knife and axe. You'll lose nine times out of ten. They learn how to fight and ride and kill from the time they are four years old. They have to be good. We've got better weapons, better horses, and more manpower. Give the Sioux what we have and we'd be back in Omaha within a year."

"Bunch of nonsense," a new voice said. Everyone turned. Major Templeton crowded into the circle of uniforms. "Goddamned nonsense. The Sioux ain't warriors. Them savages don't know how to fight a lick. Got no discipline. Every one of them damned hostiles runs around and fights when and where he wants to. When they attack a ranch, they figure to come at it from two sides. So they split up and half go over by the barn and the other half by the house. They're supposed to attack at dawn, except these two warriors see twelve horses in the corral. Hell, they don't wait for nobody. They sneak in, let the horses out, and then whoop and shout and chase the horses off claiming them as their personal property. Horses, that's all the Sioux want."

Everyone around the circle was quiet.

"What about man to man, Major Templeton?" Powell asked. "Could you kill a Sioux one on one if both of you had the same weapons?"

"Damn right. With a pistol, rifle . . ."

"What about a knife, an eight-inch fighting knife?" Powell pressed.

"Hell, I ain't too good with a blade." Templeton looked around at the group of officers. "But hell, when are we one on one? You give me eighty good cavalry-men, and I'll wade right through the whole goddamned Sioux nation!"

There was a moment of stunned silence.

"You really mean that, Major?" a First Lieutenant asked.

"Hell yes. Give me eighty fully-equipped men, trained, good shots, and good horses, and I'll wade across Sioux land and turn it into a damn desert." "Major, don't you think that a Sioux arrow or lance could sink into your chest as easily as anyone's?" Colonel Cavanaugh asked. "I've seen some mighty brave and strong men take an Indian arrow and die in minutes. The Sioux use those big buffalo hunting arrows that are sharply pointed and an inch wide at the tail. In fact, these days most of the Sioux make metal points for their war arrows."

"Don't matter none to me. Damn Sioux got to get within fifty yards to do much damage with them arrows. My Henry will reach out damn near a mile and kill the bastards."

"I've never seen a Sioux yet, Major, who I can keep a mile away," Cavanaugh smiled. "They're sneaky. Now I know you saw some combat at the end of the Civil War, but I'm not sure how much actual fighting you've done against the Sioux."

"Three damn years of building this fort we had to fight off the Sioux and some Cheyenne damn near every day, Colonel. I've had my share of shooting Indians. I still say, you give me eighty good men and I'll make mincemeat out of the damn Sioux nation." Now that he had everyone's ear, Templeton continued. "What we really need is to respond to these attacks. When ten Sioux attack our wood train, we should rescue the crew, sure. But then we should take two hundred men, chase down the hostiles, and kill every one of them. Chase them back to their camp, burn down their villages, smash their pots, and destroy their food. We need to exterminate the bastards!"

"Major, you know we have to go by our orders," Cavanaugh replied smoothly. "And we're under orders to make a measured response to attacks. We don't have the manpower to launch seize-and-destroy campaigns against the Sioux."

"Damn shame. Damn shame," the major muttered, reeling away and stumbling into a chair.

"Dinner time! It's dinner time! You boys stop playing soldier and come in to the table." It was their hostess, Virginia Whipple, calling. The men cut off their army talk and moved sedately toward the table, looking for their name cards on the plates. Soon, the officers and their wives were seated, with Colonel Cavanaugh at the head of the long table. There were seventeen altogether. The meal began.

On Cavanaugh's right sat Virginia Whipple. She was big and buxom, a blonde with a New England accent and a dress cut low enough to show a sharp cleavage. She kept Cavanaugh busy with small talk most of the meal.

On Cavanaugh's other side sat Martha Hines, wife of the surgeon, Captain Hiram Hines. She was small and quiet, and spoke only when spoken to.

Cavanaugh attempted to evaluate the men as he watched and listened, but Virginia Whipple broke in at the most inopportune times, frustrating him. At last he gave up and talked to her. She was from New York. This was her tenth army post, and she was looking forward to staying at Fort Keogh for a long time. Marcus ate automatically, and was glad when the dessert came, cherry pie with fresh whipped cream. He didn't know how they could keep the cream fresh so long from that one old cow.

Soon the dinner was over. The men cleared back the table and rolled up the rug for dancing. Two of the officers had teenaged daughters who joined the party. Two fiddlers provided music and set a lively pace. Cavanaugh danced one set with each of the six ladies, then sat out to talk with his officers again. Before long, Major Templeton and Captain Whipple, who had been second-in-command under Templeton, pushed into the group. For a half hour they talked of Indian fighting, of army posts, and army foul-ups.

Then Major Templeton stood up, weaving slightly. For a while the food had sobered him, but additional drink was doing its work. "I still don't understand the army. Been in it all my life. Gave four years of my life here building this damn fort. It's good. I'm good. Why the hell they dumping me out and moving me down a step? I want somebody to explain it to me."

He looked around the group of six or seven officers. There was an uncomfortable silence. At last Lieutenant Powell cleared his throat.

"Sir, I don't see it as any kind of a demotion. Hell, you're still here, and as second-in-command you'll have a lot to do with running the fort. You concentrated on engineering for a lot of years, right? Maybe the army wants you for another fort somewhere, maybe up in the Rocky Mountains or down in Arizona somewhere against them damn Apaches." Templeton stared at Powell.

"Hell no. Just shit on me is what the army did. Right in my face. Must want me to resign. Hell, so we're losing the fight against the Sioux up here. Army brass knows we're on a short string. No way we can keep these northwest trails open if the Sioux want them closed. Fact is, I hear we got men out talking to the damn Sioux right now, making a deal to close down Fort Keogh. Close it down, move out, and leave it to the Sioux. I'll guarantee you one thing. We walk away from Keogh, the damn Sioux will have it set on fire before we're fifty yards away. They hope the buffalo will come back, but they won't. The Big Fifties done too much hurt to the herds. Buffs never gonna come back like they was."

Colonel Cavanaugh looked around. Some of the

men were beginning to look tired, but they were duty bound to stay until he left.

"The army still needs Fort Keogh. General Sheridan has been quite clear on that score," Colonel Cavanaugh told them. "He wants to make sure we keep it. I'm going to bust my head to try to get more men. We should have eight hundred here at least. Then we'd have enough men to send out two hundred at a time to pursue and catch the Sioux, burn their villages, and drive them north."

"Them Sioux ain't that vicious. You give me my eighty men, lots of ammo, and good horses," Major Templeton said, repeating his earlier words—this time with a noticeable slur. "Hell, I'll wade right through the whole damn Sioux nation. You remember that!" The disgruntled officer lifted his brows, and with a great sigh, slumped forward over the table and passed out.

4

CHIEF WHITE EAGLE SAT IN HIS TIPI ON THE POWDER River, forty miles from the pony soldiers' fort at Pine Woods. Chief White Eagle had lived nearly thirty-five summers and was war chief of the Ogalala Sioux band that bore his name. He had nearly eighty tipis spread out along the Powder, and could put seventy-five warriors into the field to fight. Scattered over ten miles up and down the river were more than two thousand tipis, gathered in a confederation with the single purpose of driving the White Eyes out of the fort on Piney Creek. Then it would be burned to the ground, and the valleys of the Powder, as well as the Tongue and Rosebud rivers, would draw the buffalo again so hunting would be good.

Delicate treaties had been made with other bands in the area: The Miniconjous, Unkpapas, Brules, and Sans Arcs Sioux all gathered for the important fight.

They had met in a great war council, and White Eagle of the Ogalalas had been named their war chief.

The first snow of the year drifted down outside. Chief White Eagle waited for the other war chiefs to assemble for the overall plan of attack. He was warm and secure in his buffalo-skin-covered tipi. The bottoms of each side had been turned in, with beds and parfletches holding the skins down to make the tipi warm and snow-proof. A dozen strips of buffalo jerky from the last hunt hung from rawhide to one side. A warming fire burned in the fire pit in the center of the tipi, and smoke rose through the opening at the top. White Eagle's three wives rested on their beds at the far side of the tipi, well out of the way.

The chiefs had talked of making two major attacks on the pony soldiers, one at Pine Woods, which the White Eyes called Fort Keogh, and the other one at Big Horn, farther up the Westward Trail.

The entrance flap on the big tipi was. open, signi-fying that visitors were welcome to come inside. One by one, the war chiefs arrived, entering the tipi on the right. They passed behind their host and went around to the far side of the fire, where they stood until their host greeted them. Then the chiefs seated themselves around the fire. Old friends and cousins talked as the chiefs gathered. When all twenty were there, Chief White Eagle lifted his hand and began to speak.

"It is good that we come together to rout the Round-eye soldiers from Pine Woods. It is the Time of

Snows, and even now the first begins. No longer is the Time of Snows a period when the Sioux People can sit in their tipis and dream of the Time of New Grass. Instead we must fight and win. For the past few months we have been fighting the Round Eyes when they go cut wood to take back to their fort. Without the wood they will freeze. My plan is to continue to attack the woodcutters with forty or fifty warriors. We will create problems for them, kill as many as we can. That is only the first move."

He paused and looked around to see that his words were sinking in. "What we wait for is the rescue force, which is always sent out from the fort when we attack the men cutting wood. When the larger force comes, we will decoy it into our trap and kill every pony soldier they send against us. It will be a great victory and it will make the White Eye generals know that we are strong. They will abandon the fort at Pine Woods and the buffalo will come again."

A murmur of assent rose from the gathered chiefs. White Eagle waited a moment, and spoke again.

"It may take us several days of raids on the wood-cutters before the Round Eyes send out a large rescue force to fall into our trap. We are patient. We can wait for the White Eye general, who will ride into our trap with all of his men. Then we will fall upon them and kill them, and take their horses and long guns and return to our tipis. The pony soldiers will see our strength and abandon their puny fort. It will be good."

In the best democratic tradition, each of those present was allowed to talk for or against the plan, for as long as he wished. A council as large as this might last all night and all the next day as well.

Running Bear of the Brules spoke first. "How big is this large force of White Eyes you speak of? Is it a hundred of their warriors? How many warriors are at the fort at Pine Woods? How can we be sure that by losing one rescue force the pony soldiers will give up this fort they have worked so hard to build?"

Another voice came, endorsing White Eagle's plan. The speaker was one of the Unkpapas. "It is good. We will wait for woodcutters and kill them, and wait for more of the pony soldiers to come out of the fort and kill them, too. Soon they will use up their wood and burn the buildings to stay warm. Then they will tramp through the snow south and east, and we will be free of the Round Eyes. Then the buffalo will come back. It is good."

"It is not a good plan." As he spoke, Running Wolf walked back and forth in front of the fire, catching the eyes of the chiefs. "We want a big fight with the Pine Woods fort. This is a little fight. Yes, it is good to decoy the White Eyes into a trap. After they are all dead we should wait for the pony soldiers to find them, and set upon them when they recover their dead. Then it will be easier for our two thousand warriors to ride to the Pine Woods fort itself and set it on fire, rout the White Eyes, and force them to the east. We must drive them into the cold and snow as they have done to our people. We must attack the fort at Pine Woods or this small fight will do no good."

The talk went on and on. Some of the chiefs had made up their minds about the plan. Others debated a long time, not sure which side they were on. Wood had to be added to the fire three times more before the last speaker had his say. Chief White Eagle listened to the silence for the time a fly would take to buzz around the inside of the tipi. When no voice rose to discuss the war plan, the chief took out the pipe he had held, lighted the bowl, and lifted it high so all could see. Then he lowered it, drew, and puffed four times as was his right. He passed the pipe to the man next to him.

Every chief had his chance at the pipe. If he agreed with the plan, he remained seated and smoked two or more puffs and passed the pipe. If he did not agree he would stand and refuse to smoke.

When the pipe had made the rounds and come back to Chief White Eagle, he counted the chiefs standing. Fifteen had smoked the pipe. The plan was approved.

"It is good," Chief White Eagle said. "We will meet in three days here to work out our plans. Within one hand of days after that, we will be on the move to set up a war camp only a few miles from the woodcutters of the fort at Pine Woods." Chief White Eagle said good-bye to the war chiefs from the other bands and sighed. He had convinced most of them of the sound-ness of his plan, but there would be trouble with Running Wolf. He was young and ambitious. He thought the Sioux were stronger than they actually were.

If the pony soldiers made an all-out campaign, they could put a thousand troops on the Powder River with cannon and rifles, and the Sioux would be driven into the far hills with no horses, no food, and no water. They had to force the pony soldiers back, but only a little at a time so the Great White Father in Washington did not become enraged and send five thousand troops after the Sioux.

Many Skies, White Eagle's first wife, came out from the darkness and put more wood on the warming fire. They would keep it burning tonight. It was the Time of the Snows and it would cover the earth until the grass was new.

Many Skies filled his pipe and he smoked again, watching the wood in the fire burn to ash. He recalled the days of his youth when there were no pony soldiers. The White Eyes were heard about but never seen, because most of them were far away toward the rising sun. It had been the days of the buffalo, when the great beasts roamed the prairies, turning the green grass into a brown wave with thousands and thousands of the creatures. It had been good.

Now there was anger. There were White Eyes everywhere, and the buffalo were almost gone. There was talk of treaties and reservations. There was pain, sickness, and death.

Many Skies rubbed her husband's shoulder, which had been wounded two summers ago. It hurt him in the cold weather. She knew that White Eagle was the war chief of the whole Sioux nation for this fight. Many Skies was proud. She knelt beside him.

"There will be trouble with Running Wolf," he told her. "The young man is ambitious, but he is also wild and does not think through what he is about to do."

"You will convince him."

"He refuses to be convinced. He may challenge me."

Many Skies rubbed his shoulder harder. "He is younger, stronger. You must convince him. You are White Eagle with powerful medicine against the White Eyes. No rifle bullet has ever harmed you. You have been in many fights with the pony soldiers and even the rifle that fires many times cannot hurt you. Running Wolf can't argue against this."

"He will. I saw how he is. He would use anything to challenge me. It is his way." The chief stood. "Now it is time for my purification rites. I must remain pure and strong for the coming fight. Nothing must interfere."

"But it is snowing outside."

"The great spirit knows it is snowing. Still the rite must be performed." Chief White Eagle stripped off the buckskin shirt he wore against the cold, and pulled off the leggings and moccasins made of three layers of leather with insulation between them. He stripped down to his breechclout.

Many Skies frowned and held her hands to the fire. "Surely the spirits would not ask you to do this." "Do not say that, wife. Get to your bed, I'll be back soon and need warming."

He lifted the flap of the tipi and stepped into three inches of fresh snow. Without flinching from the near freezing temperature, Chief White Eagle walked barefoot a quarter of a mile to his prayer rock. It had taken him two days to find it since their last move. Now he knelt on the rock and lifted his hands to the falling snow.

He made his long prayer to the spirits of the hunt and of war. Then he lay facedown on the snow-covered rock, and for a moment he shivered. For thirty minutes he lay in the snow, praying to the spirits to cleanse him in body and mind. When it was time to leave, his left arm would not work correctly. The chill had affected his shoulder where he had the war-axe wound. Chief White Eagle held his left arm carefully and returned to his tipi.

Many Skies had kept the fire going. She was at his side at once with his warmest buffalo robe. She put it around his shoulders, saw him cradling his left arm, and frowned. He sat before the fire and slowly warmed. Many Skies massaged his shoulder through the buffalo robe. It soon returned to normal.

When he could use his arm again and stopped shivering, he nodded at his first wife. "Let me warm your bed, Many Skies. It has been too many days." They slid into the bed Many Skies had kept warm with rocks from near the fire, and Chief White Eagle made love with his first wife.

The next morning, White Eagle pondered his problem. It would not come to a serious confrontation for another three days, when the chiefs were to gather again. White Eagle thought through the plan, as well as the arguments for and against it. It was a good plan, and it would work. If Running Wolf did not agree with him and wanted to challenge his leadership, it would be his choice.

White Eagle began work on a new lance he was making. It was twelve feet long and tipped with a metal point as long as his hand. He had formed and pounded the metal with a hammer he took from a settler. Then he sharpened the metal point with the flat metal the White Eyes called a file. Soon he would have the sharpest, most deadly lance in the entire Sioux nation.

He hefted the lance, looked outside, and saw that the snow had risen more than a foot. It had stopped for a short time, but by the looks of the sky it would snow again, probably for two more days.

Chief White Eagle went back inside his tipi and put more wood on the fire. What good would a fine lance do him if he was dead by the time of the attack?

The challenge to his status as a war leader didn't happen very often. It could be a polite contest to see who could throw a war axe with the most accuracy. It could be political, someone could challenge his right to be war leader.

Or the challenge could turn deadly and become a contest of survival, with the participants using bows and arrows, spears, war axes or knives in a fight to the death. The man who was challenged had the choice of the weapons. He could choose a throwing contest or a fight to the death.

White Eagle pulled his warmest buffalo robe around his shoulders and put on a felt hat he had brought back from a raid. He stalked outside. He walked a mile up the river, through the snow that drifted through the trees, past dozens of tipis. Then he retraced his steps. By the time he got back, he still had not made up his mind what kind of a fight it would be with Running Wolf. All he knew was that he was sure there would be a challenge.

Inside his tipi, his three children romped around the fire. His two sons were four and six summers. They would be fine Sioux warriors one day. He must make certain they had that chance by keeping the traditional Sioux hunting grounds safe for the buffalo.

A Sioux warrior did not romp and play with his children, at least not when others could see. But White Eagle loved his sons and spent much time with them, showing them how to carve and hunt, and ways they could use a knife in impromptu fighting. Both boys had been learning how to be Sioux warriors since they were three. Already the six-year-old was surprisingly accurate with the small bow that White Eagle had made for him. Soon he would get a larger, stronger bow to shoot birds and squirrels for the cooking pot. White Eagle smiled. It was good.

In his tipi five miles downstream, in the camp of the Unkpapas, Running Wolf looked outside his tipi and swore mightily at the weather. Snow! Exactly what he didn't want for the big fight with the White Eyes. Snow would slow them down, make it easier to track them. It would be much easier for the pony soldiers to see them coming and to sound an alarm.

Winter was not the time to fight!

He picked up his favorite knife, a hunting knife he had found on a raid against a ranch, and stalked outside. The snow was more than a foot deep in the open. He went under the pines, found a sturdy tree, and paced off ten long steps. There he drew a line in the snow and hefted his knife.

In one fluid motion, he brought the blade back and threw it at the pine tree. The big knife spun once and stuck in the heavy bark of the pine.

Running Wolf grunted, walked forward, and retrieved the knife. Then he cut a short stick and sharpened the end. He found a broad maple tree leaf and pinned it to the pine with the sharp peg which he drove in with the handle of his knife.

He could stick the knife in the tree every time— that wasn't the problem. If he challenged Chief White Eagle, the chief would have the right to select the contest and he was certain the Ogalala would select knives, a contest of throwing knives. That was because it was well known that Chief White Eagle was a master in using a knife. Running Wolf, on the other hand, was better with the hatchet or war axe.

For two hours, Running Wolf practiced throwing his knife into the tree. Twice he cut up the maple leaf so much he had to put up a new one. It was said that

White Eagle could split the shaft of an arrow when it was pinned sideways against a tree. He could do this at thirty feet, and split an arrow nine times out of ten.

Running Wolf took his knife and walked back to his tipi. If he beat White Eagle now, he would do so in front of twenty chiefs from the Sioux nation. It would make him the new war chief for the big fight at Pine Woods! But if he lost, he would die.

It didn't seem likely. The chief was known for his sound judgement and intelligence. Running Wolf stared at his wife of three years, Gentle Fawn. She was heavy with child. He would soon be a father. It was a great responsibility. Children came infrequently in the Sioux nation. The women worked hard and some said that was the reason it was hard for them to get pregnant. He knew that the White Eyes bred like rabbits. Some of the ranches they had raided had ten or twelve children from one wife!

Gentle Fawn looked up at him as if to say something, but he scowled and she turned away. She was only a woman. Her job was to work and take care of her warrior and provide him with three sons. That was a wife's job. If he won the contest with White Eagle, he would take another wife. With Gentle Fawn ready to bring forth, he would not be able to use her for at least three years.

It was the custom of his people for the mothers to breastfeed their children to the age of three or four. No intercourse was allowed while the wife suckled her baby. He looked at his wife's swollen body and longed for a slender woman he could bed. He would start today to look for a second wife. He had over fifty ponies and war horses. It was time.

His thoughts went back to the approaching battle. Killing a few, even a hundred White Eyes from the fort would not make them close up and run away. He knew that. Why didn't the council of chiefs understand? With two thousand warriors, they could attack the fort and overwhelm it. The plan to drain off their manpower and use the woodcutters as a way to draw a large-sized rescue force into a trap was good.

But after the first kill, they should either wait for more rescuers to come so they could kill them as well, or attack the fort directly. Then he knew his strategy.

He would propose that they follow White Eagle's plan, only add to it. As soon as they succeeded in wiping out a rescue force, they could shift most of their manpower and wait for a second rescue team to leave the fort. A hidden force would attack the second rescue force. With the fort low on fighting soldiers, the main body of the Sioux would attack the Pine Hills fort itself. Then they would burn it to the ground and capture the horses that were there. It was a move that would set the White Eyes and the pony soldiers back on their haunches for many summers.

Running Wolf warmed himself over the fire, then went back to his target tree and threw his six-inch-bladed hunting knife two hundred more times. For the last ten he drove the blade cleanly into the small oak-tree leaf he had fixed as a target.

Running Wolf hurried back to his tipi. Now he was sure that he would challenge White Eagle at the next council. He guessed that White Eagle would make it a friendly contest of knife throwing. If he defeated White Eagle, then he would be the war chief.

5

BY THE DAY OF THE MEETING WITH THE TWENTY CHIEFS, there was two feet of snow on the ground. Chief White Eagle welcomed the leaders into his tipi.

"It will be easier for us now," said Chief Longbow from the Miniconjous. "We well be able to butcher them easily as the White-eye soldiers struggle through the snow."

There were murmurs of approval. Running Wolf rose and looked at White Eagle.

"Great warriors, I have a proposal to make. It has to do with our attack on the Pine Woods fort."

There were a few murmurs of disapproval from the war chiefs. The matter had been settled already. White Eagle gave a curt motion with his hand for the Unkpapas chief to continue.

"What is Running Wolfs proposal?"

The younger warrior outlined his plan. After the first ambushes, as White Eagle had proposed, with the fort drained of its fighting men, some 1500 Sioux would attack and overwhelm the stockade. When Running Wolf finished, he looked around.

Silently, White Eagle stood up, indicating his disapproval. One by one, others joined him, until fifteen of the chiefs were standing. Running Wolfs idea was not accepted by the council. When the war chiefs all sat down again, Running Wolf rose and walked in front of White Eagle.

"You are an old man with old ideas. You have no thoughts of winning, only striking and running away like an angry dog. You are not a Sioux warrior." Running Wolf tossed a buffalo arrow in White Eagle's lap. "I challenge you for your right to lead this council. I declare that such challenge be satisfied tomorrow morning, so we can quickly attack the fort at Pine Woods."

White Eagle stood majestically, took the arrow in both hands, and broke it in half. He threw it at Running Wolfs feet. He accepted the challenge. Then he turned and marched outside. The council session was over. It would resume after combat, when the war chief of the Sioux nation was decided.

White Eagle returned to his tipi when Running Wolf had gone. Gray Fox of the Sans Arcs spoke to him.

"My friend, this is a serious challenge. It must be dealt with quickly and with force."

"I know, Gray Fox. I have suspected it since our last meeting. It will be met with due force."

Elk Tooth, the oldest of the war chiefs and an Ogalala, limped to his host and put his hands on White Eagle's shoulders. "Let there be no anger. I bounced you on my knee when you were a scrub pine.

This is a small matter, White Eagle. Do not let it become large. Surely this is not anything worth dying for. Let us keep our blood-letting for the enemy. Think well on it, my young warrior chief."

White Eagle asked six of his closest friends on the council to remain in his tipi. The others politely left to find shelter with others among the Ogalala band or returned to their own tipis. The seven remaining men sat around the fire in White Eagle's lodge. They began to talk about the idea of attacking the fort. It was agreed that the deep snow would work against them. They needed the ability to attack quickly and retreat if necessary.

"The pony soldiers at the fort have the big guns that can shoot a giant ball of iron or throw out a thousand arrowheads all at once. One shot can kill fifty warriors!"

"There are six or eight such guns at the White Eyes' fort," Running Bear of the Brules said. "One of my men was near the fort one day and. saw them. If the deep snow slows us down, many will die."

Many Skies brought out a rabbit stew that had been simmering on the warming fire. There was enough for all. White Eagle invited his six friends to spend the night in his lodge, but all declined.

"You will have work enough to do tonight with

your three wives," Gray Fox teased him. "Each wife must be satisfied before a challenge can be met." The men drifted off to other tipis where they would be welcomed. When they had gone, Many Skies knelt by White Eagle near the fire.

"The challenge, it is a small thing, isn't it, my husband?"

"No, it's not a small thing, Many Skies. This young chief has long wanted to be war chief of all the Sioux.

He is ambitious, but he is not wise enough or worthy to be war chief. It is my job to make sure that he does not win the challenge tomorrow."

"So you will make the contest knife throwing," Many Skies said, showing her delight. "There is no warrior in all the Sioux nation who can throw a knife better than you can."

"That may be. But since Running Wolf knew he would challenge me, he has been practicing his knife throwing. He will be ready. I must make the challenge something else. It must be a surprise for Running Wolf. Such an important challenge must be known by the spirits. Perhaps they will speak to me tonight on my prayer rock."

Many Skies touched White Eagle on the chest. "My husband, with you it has been a good marriage, a fine life. I do not wish to start over with a new husband. I know the ways of warriors. You must show how strong and mighty you are." A tear crept from her eye and rolled down her cheek. "I do not care if you are mighty or not. Make it an easy challenge. Do not make me wail and weep at your funeral tomorrow night. I'm too young to be a widow."

White Eagle smiled and held her face in his hands. He kissed her lips and held her close.

"Many Skies, I will do tomorrow what I must do as the war chief of all the warriors of the Sioux nation. It will be right and it will be just, and I shall not die. I will talk with the spirits tonight."

"But you will be with me tonight?" she asked.

"I will be with each of you. It is the way of the People. Let me sit and watch the fire. Sometimes I see the spirit of the fire in the leaping flames and she talks to me."

Late in the afternoon, White Eagle went to his prayer rock. He sat there until it became dark, then stripped down to his breechcloth and fell facedown on the rock. At first the ice numbed his nearly naked body, but as he lay there with his arms outstretched, he began to feel warmth. Ahead of him he saw a figure, a warrior chiseled in white light moving toward him. He tried to cry out, but could not. He closed his eyes, but still the warrior strode toward him through the darkness.

A moment later, the man was beside him. He raised White Eagle up and put his fighting knife on the war chiefs shoulder. He spoke, not with a voice, but directly into White Eagle's mind.

"Great warrior, tomorrow you will meet and defeat this puny enemy. You will use your favorite weapon, for this young one has the mark of the black spirit, and he will bring the Sioux nation to ruin if he is allowed to lead. He must be stopped for all time."

Slowly the warrior faded into the blackness of the night. White Eagle found himself prostrate over the prayer rock. His flesh was warm, even where he had been on the ice. He sat up, dressed, and returned to the lodge.

"It is the way of the spirits," he whispered to himself. Then he began to make final preparations for the battle. He took out his eight-inch fighting knife. With a sharpening stone he honed it to a sharpness that cut a hair.

Then he put away the knife, made sure his lance, bow and arrows, and shield were just inside the tipi where he could grab them quickly to defend the village if he needed to. He moved to the bed of his third wife. She smiled at him and lifted the buffalo robe. She was naked already, young and slender and beautiful. He would be with each of his wives tonight, for if tomorrow was to be his last day, his widows would have a last memory. It was the way of the People.

The next morning dawned cold and clouds lumbered overhead on a soft winter wind. White Eagle looked at the sky and went back inside to warm himself over the small fire in his tipi. As on any important battle, he did not eat or touch his wives the day he left. He drank water sparingly, and stretched. The challenge was set for an hour after sunrise. He heard people going past his tipi on the way to the outdoor council fire. A place had been trampled down in the snow for the combatants, and one path led to a large tree. He had asked for this so that Running Wolf would assume that the contest would be knife throwing.

He pushed the big knife in his breechclout scabbard. His wives stood by the flap as he approached. He stopped and looked at each one sternly, yet could not touch them. Then he hurried outside, wearing only his breechclout and his heavy moccasins. He carried a strip of rawhide as wide as his thumb and as long as his arm. On each end he had tied a stick of green wood the size of his small finger. He carried the rawhide rolled up and out of sight in his hand.

Already most of the people from his band had gathered around the council fire. Running Wolf stood at the side of a large, trampled circle, wearing only his breechclout and moccasins. As the challenger, he walked to the center of the circle and lifted his fist into the air straight over his head. He brought it down and pointed his fist at White Eagle. A hush fell over the crowd, which numbered more than two hundred.

White Eagle walked to the center of the circle and stopped six feet from his challenger. They stared at one another. White Eagle drew his knife from the small scabbard on his breechclout, raised it to the sky spirit, then lowered it and pointed it at Running Wolf.

Running Wolf drew his knife and pointed it at White Eagle.

White Eagle opened his left hand, letting the strip of rawhide fall and hang in the air. The onlookers gasped, and a tremor of excited chatter flamed through the crowd. Everyone knew the significance of the thong with the sticks on the end. It was to be a knife fight, not to the first blood, but to the death.

White Eagle put the small, green stick in his mouth and clamped his teeth on it. With his left hand he held out the other end of the rawhide.

It was a point of decision. The challenger could still back off and end the challenge. He would have to leave his band in disgrace and join another one as a simple warrior who would never again be allowed to attain any rank of leadership.

Or he could fight.

Running Wolf stared at White Eagle. It was too late. He reached out and caught the stick at the end of the rawhide strip, and drew it to him.

A murmur rippled through the crowd.

Running Wolf thrust the stick in his mouth and bit down on it with all his strength. The rawhide held the fighters within arm's length of each other. The two men eased backward until the thong was tight. There was no place to run, no way to escape. It was fight or die. They lifted their knives eye height. Both gave a guttural roar and the fight began.

They circled, slashing at arms and thighs. No one hit. The younger man had more stamina and would try to wear down his older opponent. White Eagle had no intention of letting that happen. He sidestepped quickly to avoid the shiny blade. The stick in his mouth jerked hard at his teeth but he held on. To drop it would mean disgrace, and his opponent would have the right to inflict a crippling slash or even a death stroke.

White Eagle stumbled, and threw his knife hand upward to catch his balance. Running Wolf reacted with the swiftness of a striking rattlesnake. His knife flashed forward. White Eagle barely had time to throw out his left arm. It took the slash that would otherwise have cut him deeply across his chest. The knife grated to the bone of White Eagle's forearm. He gasped with pain and moved back the length of the rawhide.

Blood flowed down his arm and dripped from his elbow. Another slash like that and he would collapse from loss of blood in only a few minutes. He knew he must go on the attack. He drove forward, stabbed at the smaller knife with his heavier one and smashed it aside. He drew blood from his opponent's arm, but the cut was not as deep as his own.

The fighters parried, feinted, and recovered. They kept their teeth tightly closed, panting through their mouth and nose. In the cold air their breath made puffs of steam. Again they circled, the rawhide thong tight between them. Blood ran down Running Wolf's arm and dripped into the white snow. They circled first one way, then the other, the knives poised, each man ready for any small move that would allow an opening.

Both were tiring. The younger man became impatient. He saw a slight opening and darted forward. Reacting quickly, White Eagle closed in. Running Wolf slashed three times. The first two missed but the third struck flesh, slicing White Eagle's right arm above his wrist. He almost dropped the blade.

They jumped back and eyed each other. White Eagle shifted his knife to his left and saw a gleam of victory on Running Wolfs face. The challenger knew his opponent's hand would not hold up much longer. He slashed in, then darted back without striking. Twice more he made the same move to test how White Eagle defended the move.

White Eagle did a double feint with the blade and drove forward, slicing the other man a second time on his left arm. Running Wolf looked at the new wound in amazement. Anger flooded his eyes and he hissed in fury. He feinted one way, then made a direct forward thrust.

White Eagle thrust his right arm out to take the blade. As the steel sliced into his forearm, he powered his arm upward, lifting Running Wolfs knife and his whole arm up and exposing his chest. In a continuous motion that his challenger had no chance to defend, White Eagle lunged forward. His blade drove deeply into Running Wolfs chest.

The younger man grunted. The knife fell from his fingers and he stiffened, the stick dropping from his mouth. White Eagle jerked his blade from the body of the wounded warrior. Running Wolf dropped to his knees, both hands trying to cover the stab wound in his chest. He looked up at White Eagle, his eyes growing cloudy. Then he fell over sideways, dead in the snow.

White Eagle stood looking down at the dead foe,

then pushed his own knife in his sheath and walked slowly toward the edge of the fighting ring. A great wailing rose from the women of the Ogalala band of White Eagle. They mourned the dead of any Sioux band.

Many Skies went to White Eagle's side. She had a poultice for his cuts, and, with long strips of chewed doeskin, wrapped up his two deep slashes to keep them from bleeding. He let the woman bind his wounds. His number two woman brought him a buckskin shirt, his leggings, and a warm buffalo robe.

He donned them, and then looked around for the members of the war council. He made sign language for them to come to his tipi and then began walking in that direction, a sudden weariness crashing down on him.

He had risked everything, but the spirit of the night had told him to do so. The spirit had been right. Now the plan would go ahead as set. They would win a great victory, and they would drive the pony soldiers from their ancient buffalo range.

The war council arrived. The chiefs would follow White Eagle in any battle now. He looked up as the last of the war chiefs sat down near a large warming fire and met their gaze. Solemnly, he told them, "Now it is time for us to fight the Pine Woods soldiers."

6

Lieutenant Colonel Marcus Cavanaugh looked out his window onto the parade grounds between the officers' quarters. The snow was piling up. Soon the only activity they could manage would be the wood-cutting detail. That was a major necessity now that winter had settled in.

It had been snowing almost every day since he arrived two weeks earlier. The white stuff had drifted halfway up the palisades around the fort. The wood-cutting detail went out each day. Its job was to cut logs at the pinery and haul them back to the fort where they were cut with cross-cut saws and split into firewood for the voracious appetites of the dozens of wood stoves on the post.

Yesterday the wood-lot sergeant had determined that the wood brought in daily was equal to what burned daily. It was all they could do to keep the supply up. For the next several months, most soldiering at Fort Keogh would come to a halt. Little could be done anyway when everything was frozen solid or under three feet of snow.

Cavanaugh was familiar with the outstanding results of some of the winter campaigns on the southern plains. The troops had marched through two feet of drifted snow and heroically wiped out several bands of hostiles, driving the survivors to containment on reservations.

Cavanaugh had also seen reports that showed the losses. One group of three companies of cavalry had become lost in a series of small hills and gullies in snow three feet deep. By the time the units were found, all but five or six of the horses had been put down and half of the men were unfit to fight for two months.

In the two weeks since he'd taken command of Fort Keogh, Cavanaugh had talked privately with each of the officers, moved one man from a spot he was determined to leave, and made him happy with a new position. The rest seemed quite comfortable in their assignments, with the exception of Major Templeton and his lackey, Captain Whipple. They continued to stir up trouble, but the new commander had been stern. He demanded unswerving loyalty to his command. Any attempt at undercutting his position with the other officers or with the troopers would be dealt with as harshly as the regulations allowed, including court martial for insubordination if necessary.

His main concern was the wood detail, which was

taking more manpower than it should. Every day they sent four wagons to the pinery. That was the best spot to get logs for firewood. It was about three miles away on a densely-forested slope of a hill, and easily accessible. For the past four days, the Sioux had hit the wood cutters on each trip. The first day they had twelve men felling and trimming trees for the wagons, and fifteen men standing guard. That day, thirty Sioux attacked the detail from the timber side of the hill and routed the soldiers back to the cover of the wagons.

The hostiles did not push the attack. Instead, they fired their rifles into the wagons, and sniped at the men who showed themselves. They killed one trooper that day and wounded two more on the initial attack.

The gunfire could be heard from the fort, but since it was a cloudy day, the lookout on Sullivant Hills could not respond with his flashing mirror. A relief force of fifty men were mounted and sent out. They pushed the hostiles well back into the woods, then routed them to the north toward Lone Pine Ridge trail. When the hostiles were well out of range of the wood-cutters, the relief force returned and stood guard as the men finished loading the wagons. They managed to drive them back to the fort with no more casualties.

By the fourth day, yesterday, there had been sixteen woodcutters to do the job faster and a defense force of twenty troopers. The pattern was almost identical. The hostiles seemed to have no interest in wiping out the woodcutting detail.

Officers from the rank of first and second lieutenants were assigned on a rotating basis to lead the woodcutting details, and anyone handy went out with the daily relief columns. That morning when the wood detail left, Cavanaugh sent Sergeant Major Flynn along as his personal observer.

"I want to know the intent of the damn redskins.

Why are they attacking and waiting for the reinforcements, then sashaying up toward Lone Pine Ridge trail and giving up the fight? It's mighty odd. Why don't they overwhelm the small force there and score some points?"

Now it was ten-thirty, about the same time that the Sioux had attacked the woodcutters before. If they hit them today, Colonel Cavanaugh was determined to ride out with the relief column. He had his horse ready and waiting outside his office.

Fifteen minutes later he went to the lookout position nearest the woodcutters to watch. The sky was leaden with potential snow again so the heliograph couldn't send messages by sun flashes. Five minutes after the colonel paced the wooden platform in the blockhouse near the main gate, they heard rifle fire to the west.

"There it goes again," the colonel said. He hurried down the steps, Ordered out fifty troopers who had been on alert, and rode with them out the gate. Half of them were cavalry from Lieutenant Powell's company, the rest mounted infantrymen. Captain Whipple had volunteered to take out the troops that day and no one made any objections.

Colonel Cavanaugh rode along at the head of the column with Captain Whipple. The horses and wagons had made a trail through heavy snow to the pinery. The wagons had sled runners on the boxes instead of wheels, giving them easier access over the snow and less work for the horses and mules.

The relief force officers rode quickly through the high drifts. By the time his force arrived at the fight, the Sioux had pinned down the defenders and the wood choppers behind the wagons. The hostiles were mounted, and ranged along the small hills to the east and north of the woodcutters. Once again, they did not seem to press their advantage.

Captain Whipple and Colonel Cavanaugh led the mounted men on a charge through the snow that seemed to surprise the hostiles. They held steady for a moment. The sudden, thundering fire from their rifles and carbines convinced the hostiles to break off contact and quietly retreat to the first good timber cover. They were heading along their usual route. They went toward the west end of the Sullivant Hills. Just at the edge of the hills they slid behind heavy timber and sent a volley of rifle fire at the approaching cavalry.

"Into the woods—take cover!" Cavanaugh bellowed. The troops swung into the brush and pine woods, losing sight of the hostiles. Cavanaugh worked slowly forward through the timber until he could see where the Sioux had taken to the woods. He saw the rump of an Indian war pony only half concealed, lifted his Spencer, and sent a round into the brown hide.

The pony reared and raced out of the thicket with the warrior hanging on. Half a dozen more hostiles slid out of the woods, firing behind them. They headed away from the hills and splashed across the Big Sandy River.

"Forward, men!" Cavanaugh shouted. The mounted soldiers straggled out of the brush and formed up. They charged through the heavy snow after the Sioux. The hostiles moved quickly, but didn't break off contact.

Leading the troopers, the colonel and Captain Whipple pushed the Sioux north but stopped when they came to the Lone Pine Ridge trail. Colonel Cavanaugh did not like the looks of the country beyond the trail. He could see where the well-used trail descended from the ridge, and there were many ravines on both sides covered with snow and ice. It looked like a winter nightmare.

"Half of those hostiles will be hiding down in there," Captain Whipple said.

"No sense pushing them any farther," the colonel said. "Our job is to keep those wood wagons protected so they can get loaded and back to the fort."

The rescue party returned to the woodlot area and stood guard for the next four hours while the troopers felled pine trees, cut them, and loaded up. For the return trip, the mounted force split, half in front of the wagons and half behind. The horses pulled the wagons easily over the packed snow to the fort.

Back in his office that afternoon, Colonel

Cavanaugh called Lieutenant Powell and Captain Whipple in for a conference. They drew a rough map of the pine woods area, carefully marking the ridges and rivers.

"Why are the hostiles harassing us, then pulling back only far enough to relieve the pressure? And why do they repeat the process the next day?" Colonel Cavanaugh asked.

"It makes no sense from a military point of view," Lieutenant Powell said. "The hostiles had enough men to overrun the woodcutters. Why didn't they?" "Could this be a pattern they want to build up so we'll come to expect it and react in a certain way?" Colonel Cavanaugh asked. "Later it could be used as a diversion for an all-out attack on the fort itself." "But Colonel, I've never heard of an Indian force attacking a fort of any kind, especially not one palisaded like ours is," Captain Whipple said. "There must be another reason."

They studied the map again, and at last all three shook their heads in despair.

"No logical reason I can see," Lieutenant Powell said.

"At least we can set up some standing orders regarding this particular position," Cavanaugh noted. He looked at Powell. "Lieutenant, what's your evaluation of the terrain just the other side of Lone Pine Ridge trail?"

"That's an exceeding rugged area, sir. Lots of hollows and depressions. It's partially covered by timber and would be an ideal place to hide two companies of men if we had them."

The colonel looked at Captain Whipple.

"Yes, sir. I agree. A good spot for an ambush for either side. It would be almost impossible to determine from the trail if there were any hostiles just below in that area."

"Good enough. These will be the standing orders. In case of a report of the Sioux corralling the wood wagons, or the sound of firing from the woodcutting area, a force of fifty of our best men will be dispatched to drive off the hostiles and safeguard the wood detail. They'll stand guard until their work is done and escort them back to the fort. If the hostiles are pursued, they will on no account be chased farther than the Lone Pine Ridge trail. Beyond that the terrain could hide dozens of hostiles."

Powell wrote as the colonel spoke, and when he had it down he read it back. The colonel corrected two words.

"Have that copied by the sergeant major and given to each of the post's field officers. Many more logcutting trips will be needed before we have enough wood for the rest of winter."

Colonel Cavanaugh excused the two officers and went back to appraising the sketch of a map they had drawn. The more he studied it, the more he agreed with his decision. The safety of the woodcutters was the paramount concern, not charging off into unknown lands.

That evening he had supper with the unmarried officers in their small mess. He had done so once a week since his arrival, and it had become a Friday night ritual. Tonight, Major Templeton arrived as well, and the meal proceeded normally. When it was over they gathered around the stove, pulled out cigars, and talked of war. Soon the subject of the standing order on pursuit of hostiles near the pinery came up.

"Colonel, I'm not sure that there will be a problem," Lieutenant Oberholtzer said. "Our main job is to protect the woodcutters. There's no reason we should follow the hostiles any farther than necessary to do that mission."

"I quite agree, Oberholtzer. However, in the heat of battle sometimes even an officer can be tricked if the trap is clever enough. The standing order is a bit of a memory jogger if nothing else."

Major Templeton put his boots up on the skirt of the hot stove and let his leather heat for a moment. "Colonel, I'm not at all certain that the reasoning behind such an order can be justified under all situations. You remember the age-old warfare term of situation and terrain. Everything in war depends on the situation and the terrain. Both can vastly alter the way a battle is fought, the way an approach to an objective is made. The terrain in one case might call for a company-front, cavalry charge. In another terrain, the troopers might have to get off to climb over rocks and through tangles of brush or across rushing streams just to bring the objective within sight."

"Major, I'm sure all of us studied tactics at the academy. The situation and the terrain certainly count in any battle. But we know the terrain here, and we're damn well certain of the situation. Now what's the point?"

"Simply that, Colonel," Major Templeton said. His color had risen considerably. "We can't be dead sure what the terrain might be beyond the Lone Pine Ridge trail. Since we can't be certain, how can we break off a hot chase when we have the bastards almost in our sights?"

"Because it is the prudent thing to do. You wouldn't ride off a thousand-foot cliff. You wouldn't try to jump the Missouri on your best warhorse. A good officer uses prudence and intelligence in all matters."

"Exactly, Colonel," Major Templeton said. "We use our intelligence to survey the terrain at the point where we reach the Lone Pine Ridge trail. We exercise our judgement, and do what seems most judicious in that specific situation." Templeton sat back, smiling because he had turned the commander's words around to suit himself.

Colonel Cavanaugh stood up slowly. "Major, I've no doubt that you were on the Point's debating team. Unfortunately, I don't give awards for slick arguments and fancy phrases. When I issue a standing order I don't expect it to be contradicted by my troops or my officers. I certainly don't expect insubordination from my second-in-command. You are walking a most precarious line."

A heavy silence filled the room. Cavanaugh looked around. "I repeat, this is a standing order for any man leading a relief party to the woodcutting area. No one, for any reason, will pursue the hostiles past the Lone Pine Ridge trail. That applies to majors and captains as well as first and second lieutenants. Gentlemen, I hope I make myself absolutely clear on this order."

None of the officers spoke. Few would even look him in the eye. It was obvious that Templeton had come there to stir up trouble over the order. When there was no reaction, Colonel Cavanaugh pushed back his chair, stubbed out his cigar, and walked out the door.

7

THAT SAME EVENING, SERGEANT MAJOR MIKE FLYNN pushed back from his desk in the Fort Keogh head-quarters and closed up. He went out the front door and down three buildings to the headquarters company barracks. To his surprise, a lamp burned in his room, and when he entered he found Sergeant McAnuff sitting on his bed. Three of the biggest men on post were also waiting for him.

"You're late, Flynn. Trying to impress your old friend, Cavanaugh?"

"What the hell are you doing in my room, McAnuff? Get your butt out of here and take your ass-lickers with you."

One of the big men made a move toward the sergeant major, but McAnuff raised his hand. "Oh, we're going, Flynn, but so are you. We've arranged a little party down in the stables—at the far end—where nobody will bother us for a couple of hours. You going with us easy or do we gag you and tie you up right here and carry you down there?"

Flynn knew it had been coming, but he hadn't expected it quite so soon. McAnuff had been the sergeant major at Fort Keogh for two years. He'd built up a lot of favors in that time. Flynn eyed the four big men. They could easily flatten him and carry him off.

"Do I need my knife and Colt, or is this going to be a fair fight?"

"Just as fair as you want to make it, asshole. I don't need any weapon to take you man to man."

"You just arranged yourself a beating, McAnuff. You're soft, you've got a gut, and I'll take pleasure in reducing you to a pile of shit alongside the horse turds."

McAnuff glared at him, then pointed to the door. Flynn went out, motioning the others ahead of him. They left the barracks by the end door and walked to the stables. Three more men waited there. They had cleared a spot near the farrier's shop, about twenty square feet, with a sprinkling of hay over the hard-packed ground. The seven watching were corporals and sergeants, all big, powerful men. Sergeant McAnuff grinned when he saw the expression on Flynn's face.

"To put it bluntly, Flynn, you don't stand a chance of winning." McAnuff laughed, pulling off his shirt.

He had it half off when Flynn charged him. His big Irish fists thundered into McAnuffs chin and right eye. The sergeant staggered backward. Flynn hit him three more times in the face before two of the big men jumped between them. One man held Flynn's hands and the other one slapped him in the face.

"Ain't nice to start before a man's ready," the giant said.

By then McAnuff had shed his shirt. He stood with only an undershirt on and his fists raised. He rushed up and slammed his knuckles into Flynn's unprotected stomach and then threw another right to Flynn's chin.

"Now, let the bastard go and see if he can hit me when I ain't all tangled up."

Both men stepped back from the middle of the straw-covered ring. Flynn knew he had nothing to lose. The match was conceded from the start. If McAnuff went down there would be another man, bigger than the sergeant, stepping in to continue the fight. He'd have to put down all seven of them to walk out of the stables. Grimly, he began his task.

Flynn had done his share of fighting in pubs and saloons, and behind barracks. The army had no boxing program, but he'd fought in Chicago as a civilian when he was stationed there. Bare knuckles were his specialty.

McAnuff was tougher than he looked. They traded blows from a distance, then moved in closer. Each man worked on the other's mid-section. Flynn drove another right into McAnuffs soft paunch. The sergeant grunted and tried to return the favor, but missed.

"Face it, McAnuff, you're out of shape, rusty." Flynn

pounded two more bare-knuckled fists into McAnuffs face and the former sergeant major backed up a step.

One of the three big men on the sidelines leaned on a three-foot-long two-by-four. McAnuff nodded at him and when Flynn turned to throw a punch, he slammed the two-by-four into the back of Flynn's thighs. The sergeant major yelled and almost crumpled to the floor. The pain was massive, but he beat it down.

"How'd you like that punch, Flynn?" McAnuff growled. He moved in quickly and slammed four hard hands to Flynn's face. Blood poured from his nose.

"Got to be careful who you turn your back on, Flynn. Guys get stabbed in the back all the time." Flynn shook his head. It was clear they wouldn't let him win against McAnuff. He reeled around the squared area, pretending to be more hurt than he was. He could go down now and let them kick him a few times, fake passing out, and hope they didn't stomp him to death.

"Dammit, no!" Flynn suddenly bellowed. He drove straight at McAnuff, grabbed him in a bear hug, and jolted his knee upward. It careened into his scrotum with full force, smashing both testicles against McAnuffs pelvic bones, bringing an immediate scream of pain. The former sergeant major slid to the floor. His knees came up to his chest and his hands touched his crotch. He passed out.

"Okay, you bastards, who's next?"

The man with the two-by-four walked into the arena. He swung it back and forth. "You shouldn't ought to have kicked Sarge in the nuts. He ain't gonna like that. Me, I don't neither."

The ape grunted and lumbered forward. Flynn danced back out of the way of the first vicious swing. He avoided the second and the third, forcing his opponent to give chase. He wasn't used to running and was already tiring.

The others seemed content to be spectators for the time being. On the next swing, Flynn darted forward instead of retreating. He caught the ape man off balance. The club swung past Flynn and then he was on him. He rammed a fist into the man's belly, powered an uppercut to the point of his chin, and hit him four more times in the stomach. The man's eyes went wide, and he slumped to the floor.

He stared up at Flynn. "Christ, where did you come from? Thought McAnuff was the toughest man on the post."

"Might have been before I came. Anybody else want some exercise and a boxing lesson?" Flynn asked, looking around the stable. Nobody moved.

The smallest man of the group, one who had been on the fringes and hadn't said a word, grabbed one of the three-tined pitchforks. He turned to Flynn and held the fork at port arms.

"Reckon I'm ready for some instruction, Sarge." Flynn looked at the row of pitchforks sticking in a stack of hay. He moved toward them, but the rest of the watchers stepped in front of him.

McAnuff groaned and sat up, still holding his

crotch. "Who the hell let the little shithead in?" "Thought you said it was all right," one of the big guys said..

"No damn killing. I told you all that. He beat me at my own game. Now take the sticker away from shithead there or give Sergeant Major Flynn one." One of the men shrugged, picked up a three-tined fork and tossed it to Flynn so he could catch the handle. At once the small man charged, holding the pitchfork like a lance.

Flynn grabbed the fork the wrong way, with the tines toward him, there was no time to switch it. He used the fork handle as a fighting staff. His hands gripped it near the center a foot apart.

The attacker was nearly on him. Flynn parried the pitchfork tines with one blow of the heavy handle. He dropped his aim and hit the kid in the chest with the side of the handle as he jolted past.

Both men whirled. Now Flynn had the fork turned so the tines were aimed at the other man.

"Come on, kid, come get your reward. Minute you picked up that pitchfork you were a dead man. You just haven't fallen over yet. Come and get it, kid. I'm waiting."

The soldier, a corporal with a bugler emblem on his shirt, hesitated.

"Not so much fun when the odds are even? Come on before I jam that bugle down your throat!"

The kid wavered, then charged. He stopped well

before he got to the sergeant and tossed his pitchfork away. He advanced slowly, his fist up.

Flynn feinted with the fork handle, then smashed it against the kid's side. They heard a rib crack. The trooper's face went white for a second. He shook the pain off and marched straight at Flynn.

The sergeant major dropped his own pitchfork and met the youth. He took a hard right fist to the cheek before he got through the flailing arms. With four hard, well-aimed blows, he smashed the corporal into the straw.

Flynn pointed at Sergeant McAnuff and at the corporal. "You four men, get these two over to the hospital. The sergeant was kicked by a horse, and the corporal fell on the icy walkway out by the outhouse." He put his fist on his hips. "Don't just sit there like jackasses. These two men are hurt. Now get them to the hospital if you have to carry them!"

The four men shrugged, helped the other two up, and walked them out of the stables. Flynn heaved a big sigh and sat down on a feed box. McAnuff wouldn't give him trouble anymore.

The next morning, Colonel Cavanaugh held one of his infrequent officer meetings. Every officer on the post was present except the surgeon. The ten men filled the commandant's office.

Colonel Cavanaugh faced them. "A few of my officers are not pleased with the defensive stance of this post. I want to give those men the chance to speak up and tell me what their position is."

"Why don't I start, Colonel?" Major Templeton said. "About a month ago, we received a directive from General Cooke who instructed us to strike the Indians in their winter camps. So far we haven't made a single foray. I've been wondering how the colonel is planning to carry out this directive from General Cooke."

"Situation and terrain, Major Templeton. I believe we spoke about this subject last night. General Cooke's order went out to all of the posts in his command. He did not specifically tell us here at Fort Keogh to march through four feet of snow into the Powder River camps and annihilate the savages. Right now we are not adequately staffed with officers or fighting men to launch such a campaign. When and if we get enough manpower to hold a reasonable force here for the defense of the fort, and have a troop of two to three hundred men to launch against the Sioux, then we will do so."

"And when do you expect we will receive enough men and ammunition to make that move possible?" Lieutenant Oberholtzer asked.

Colonel Cavanaugh turned to the new voice. "Not in my lifetime."

The comment brought a round of laughter.

"Not as funny as it sounds. The War Department is tightening up on supplies and on manpower. This fort was built by Major Templeton to house a thousand fighting men and officers. We have to cheat a little to get the roster up to three hundred."

Captain Whipple stood. "Sir, since we know it's

impossible to get any more men or officers here, isn't there something we can do with the ones we have? Why can't we respond when we are attacked on the wood detail? Would it be challenging operational plans, say, to set up an ambush just beyond the woodlot in the Sullivant Hills and ambush the Sioux when they came to attack our men?"

Colonel Cavanaugh nodded. "Captain Whipple, your suggestion is well founded. Such an ambush could be undertaken with a small group of men, say fifty. They could be strategically placed to provide a cross-fire on the hostiles as they approached the woodcutting area. Yes, I like the idea."

He looked at the other officers. "Gentlemen, this is what I mean by a creative discussion that focuses on what we can do instead of what there's no chance of doing. We will not be launching a two-hundred-man campaign against the Sioux on the Powder River. However, an ambush, cleverly set up and sprung at the precise moment, could be costly to the Sioux. I'll ponder on that."

The colonel went back to his big desk and sat down. "All right, we've heard ideas from two of you. What about the rest? There must be some questions or ideas lingering in the recesses of your minds. Now is the time to bring them out."

Lieutenant Powell stood. "Sir, I've read about a quick strike unit called the Lightning Company that was formed about ten years ago in Texas. As I recall, they traveled some forty pounds lighter in gear than the average cavalryman would. They were trained to travel at least six miles an hour, cover seventy miles a day, and be ready to fight when they arrived. Would it be possible to form one here for use next summer?" "Yes, I have read some of the same material. The man who first put together the Lightning Companies was then Captain Colt Harding. I think he has his first star now: His units were devastating to the Comanche in the Texas area. They can live off the land, so they need fewer rations to carry. But they are also highly trained in tracking, knife fighting, and hand-to-hand combat. Frankly, I'd love to have two full companies of Lightning Units. It's a good idea." Lieutenant Nate Brown stood. "Sir, I received a copy of your standing orders on pursuit of hostiles in the woodyard situation. It seems reasonable to me that if we have a chance to kill half a dozen Sioux by pursing them, we should have that option and use our field judgement whether or not we could complete the mission safely."

"Good, I'm glad someone brought this up. More of you have worried about this standing order than any other I've written. How many of you have traveled over the Lone Pine Ridge trail down to the old Westward Trail that swings around the ridge and crosses Potlatch Creek?" He waited as hands went up.

Six of the officers had been there. Lieutenant Brown was not one of those.

"The situation and the terrain, gentlemen. The terrain beyond the trail is a hodgepodge of rough country, little ravines, large rocks, and clumps of brush

—a hundred places where a fighting force could hide itself. I was thinking about that spot as one where we might ambush the Sioux some day. However, until we know the area better, it would be unwise to charge through there after a handful of Sioux. Next time you're up that way and there are no Sioux around, take a good look at that spot and report to me, Lieutenant Brown."

Since there were no more important points brought up after that, Colonel Cavanaugh dismissed the group. Major Templeton lingered.

"Yes, Major, stay awhile. We need to have a talk." When the other men were gone, Colonel Cavanaugh closed his office door and walked to the wall where the United States flag had been tacked to

the boards. He stared at Templeton for several seconds.

"Major Templeton, have you lost your mind? Or are you playing games that you have no chance of winning? How dare you question my judgement and my running of this fort in the presence of all of our subordinate officers?"

"Sir, I only . . ."

"Templeton, when I want your excuses I'll ask for them. Right now I have a choice of relieving you of your duties here as my second-in-command and sending you to another company, or I can ask you to transfer to another post. I'll give you every cooperation in getting a transfer."

"Sir, I have no thought of asking for a transfer. I built this fort. It's like a home to me."

Colonel Cavanaugh stormed back to his desk, took out paper and pen, and dipped the metal point in the ink.

"Therefore, since you won't ask to be transferred, I will order you back to Omaha. I will send along a report that details your attitude and your inability to work within the normal functioning of this fort. I will ask that you be reassigned from Omaha at the army's pleasure."

Major Templeton's face turned fire-red. He balled his hands into fists and shook with anger.

"Colonel, you can't do that. A report like that would be the end of my army career! It would dog me the rest of my life. I'd never get another promotion, and every new post would be leery of me. My life would be pure hell."

"Very well." Cavanaugh set his pen down. "I'll have no more insubordination. If you can make that commitment to me, I won't send in that report. But remember, you're a step and a half away from ending your army career. If I write that report, you'll be a dead man walking around in uniform."

Major Templeton bent his head down and covered his face with his hands.

"All right, Colonel. I'll do as you say. I'll cooperate. I'll bow to your directives and support your decisions. It'll kill me, but it's better than being shipped to Omaha as a malcontent. Yes, I'll stop talking about you. I've got nowhere to go. I just don't want to have to leave this fort."

Colonel Cavanaugh stood and looked down at the beaten man. "Templeton, I'd much rather have you transfer out on your own initiative. It would be better for your career, and make it easier here for me." "No, Colonel. I must stay here. I'll work at it, I promise." Cavanaugh watched him for a minute, then nodded. "All right. Tell Sergeant Flynn I need to talk to Captain Whipple."

"Whipple! Why? You going to come down hard . . ." Colonel Cavanaugh's stern look stopped Templeton. He stood up. "Yes, sir, Colonel Cavanaugh. I'll see that he gets right in here."

Ten minutes later, Captain Whipple sat in the chair beside the commander's desk.

"I like that suggestion you made, Whipple, and we just might do something along that line. That's why I'm transferring you out of quartermaster and making you C Company commander."

Whipple looked up, anger showing. "But why, sir?" "You're a field man, Whipple. You're wasted in quarter-master. We'll use a part-time man there. You have a good quartermaster sergeant?"

"Yes sir, first rate."

"Good. Move into the C Company orderly room today. You'll be in command, and Second Lieutenant

Scott will be a platoon leader. Remember, this is a promotion. There's no future in quartermaster work."

As soon as Whipple left, Colonel Cavanaugh scratched out a rough draft of a letter requesting a promotion for First Lieutenant Trevor Powell to captain. He doubted that it would go through the first time, but he'd send it to General Cooke and on to Sheridan anyway. Sheridan might push it for him. He just hoped it got through Congress.

8

Colonel Cavanaugh paused beside his sergeant major's desk and looked at the man's battered face.

"Sergeant Flynn?"

Flynn looked up, and a crooked grin spread over his features. "Yes, sir, Colonel Cavanaugh. You're wondering about my face. Craziest thing, sir. I fell down those damn stairs in my barracks."

"Fell down the stairs?"

"Yes, sir." Flynn couldn't help but broaden his grin.

"Well, that's interesting. Would it be out of place, Sergeant Major, if I asked how the other guy looked who fell down the same set of stairs at about the same time?"

"Sir, I'd guess he's in about the same shape. Damn stairs can be tricky."

"Will there be any more stairs trouble, Sergeant Major?"

"Oh, no, sir. I don't think so. Fact is, we kind of

helped each other out after we fell. I think the matter is settled."

"Good. You just watch your step on those stairs." Cavanaugh went into his office. Some men had a knack for working out serious problems the direct way. Evidently McAnuff and Flynn had a small battle with their fists. It would be nice if he and Templeton could resolve their differences out behind the stables, too, but it wasn't likely.

The talk about offensive action the day before had started Cavanaugh thinking. Last night before he went to sleep he planned a maneuver that might just work. He studied the map of the pine hills area where they cut wood, and judged the distances.

His idea was to create a pincer movement. The next time the wood train was attacked, the relief force would proceed with fifty men and charge to the rescue as usual, pursuing the hostiles on their usual escape route. But the troopers would go only far enough to make the Sioux think they were continuing the chase. They'd pursue them into the Sullivant Hills and across the Big Sandy River, forcing the hostiles up Lone Pine Ridge trail—the short cut across the ridge.

Then the main body of the relief column would swing north and west around the end of Lone Pine Ridge, and charge around the ridge. They would catch the hostiles when they came down from the trail near Potlatch Creek, where it crossed the old Westward Trail. At the same time, a detachment of cavalry would be sent from the fort out to the Westward Trail with its gentler slope. That force would come around and attack the hostiles from behind, near Potlatch Creek, completing the pincer. The Sioux would be trapped between the two forces.

It would certainly eliminate the problem of going down the slope across the Lone Pine Ridge trail. He called in Major Templeton and Captain Whipple and explained the reasoning to them.

"Should work," Whipple said. "Of course, it's all in the timing of the two movements. Give me the Westward Trail road. I'll have my men in position, waiting for the damned savages."

"Let's do it this morning," Colonel Cavanaugh said. "The snow doesn't look deep enough to cause any undue delays. If it does, it affects all parties equally. Nobody has been across the Westward Trail since the big snows, but, Templeton, you'll have a straight ride with no fighting and no holdups."

"How many men do we get?" Captain Whipple asked.

"You'll need cavalry and mounted infantry. We're running damn short on them. Captain Whipple, you take thirty men and use Lieutenant Lewiston for your second-in-command. You'll be in the blocking position at the end, so take the cavalry with the least training. Try not to push the hostiles too fast up that hill. You'll have to send a small squad halfway up the Long Pine Ridge to make the Sioux believe the whole force is chasing them."

"How many men can I have?" Templeton asked.

"Scrape up thirty. You'll need all the cavalry. Draw from Lieutenant Powell's troop and ask for his most reliable men. You pick first. We're almost sure to have another attack today. The Sioux haven't missed now in a week."

The day had dawned clear and not as cold. By ten o'clock, the sun had warmed the snow to the point where it was melting slightly. The whole fort was waiting for a signal from the heliograph on Sullivant Hills, alerting them that there was an attack underway. It came at 10:35, just before they heard the sound of rifles firing from the pinery.

Both sets of troops were saddled and waiting. They filed out the main gate and rode away in their different directions.

Major Templeton's forces slowed to a walk through the virgin snow north of the Westward Trail. Going west on the wood road, the relief column made better time. Captain Whipple worked his command as quickly as possible. He could hear the firing, and prayed that he would get there in time. His troops came within sight of the wood wagons and the bugler blew attack.

His men spread out for the last four hundred yards, cutting a swath through the eighteen inches of snow at a steady walk. Whipple estimated there were eighty to a hundred Sioux. They had left a dozen warriors with two rifles behind at strategic positions to slow down the blueshirts. After firing only a few shots, they pulled out. Soon the main bulk of the attacking Indians moved around the north end of Sullivant Hills, and headed up the trail that led to the top of Lone Pine Ridge.

Captain Whipple's men let loose a volley and peppered the retreating Sioux. When the cavalry force came to the trail up the ridge, Whipple sent six men to the top to fire at the Sioux, as if the main body of soldiers was in hot pursuit. When the Sioux were far enough away, they were to hurry back to the main party, which would be pushing north around the end of the ridge.

Captain Whipple tried to evaluate the timing. If he was moving too slowly and wasn't there when the hostiles arrived at Potlatch Creek, it would be disaster for Templeton's men. When he saw his six men returning from the ridge trail, he picked up the pace, even though the horses had to break a new trail through more than a foot of snow.

As his unit came to the end of Lone Pine Ridge, Captain Whipple paused and went ahead with one man. All he could find ahead was virgin wilderness. Potlatch Creek had two small tributaries and flowed almost due east where it crossed the Westward Trail. Captain Whipple hand signalled the command forward under Lieutenant Lewiston.

"Guess we'll work our way forward," he told Lewiston. "The hostiles are probably in those trees near the trail crossing at the creek. We'll flush them out, and then Major Templeton will come riding up from the south."

They rode, spread out now in a company front so each man would have a target directly ahead. It made a line thirty troopers long, moving forward at a steady walk through the foot-deep snow. When they were two hundred yards from Potlatch Creek and the Westward Trail, they could see movement. Indians. They picked up the pace. Suddenly fifty Indians stormed from the woods.

The left flank of the line, with Lieutenant Lewiston, was made up mostly of green men who had seen little fighting. Three men in the middle of that section turned and galloped away to the rear. Half a dozen more started to do the same thing. Lewiston fired a pistol round over their heads, turned them and held them in the end of the line. Just before they met with the hard-riding Ogalala Sioux warriors, six more of the green cavalrymen broke, galloping in pure panic to the rear, leaving Lieutenant Lewiston and Sergeant Constantine alone. Twenty warriors screeched their war cries and slanted away from the retreating horses. They kicked their war ponies to the left and surrounded the two mounted blueshirts. Within a minute, both troopers were pierced by arrows and impaled from lance thrusts.

Captain Whipple saw the bloodbath and used his pistol, firing over the men's heads. He rode hard and turned the nine men back to the main party, screaming at them to join his half of the line. They merged into an organized unit and Captain Whipple ordered them to lay down a steady hail of rifle fire at the Sioux. Without cover and only three rifles among them, the outgunned Sioux were forced to fall back.

Captain Whipple took one more look down the Westward Trail for Major Templeton. There was no sign of him. He pointed to six men and charged to the spot where he had last seen Lieutenant Lewiston. He found the two bloody bodies on the white snow. Their horses and weapons had been stolen. The troopers loaded the bodies behind their saddles and rode back to the main party.

Captain Whipple turned his men and made a strategic withdrawal, keeping up a good volley of rear-guard fire to discourage any more attacks by the Sioux.

When he was a mile away from the encounter, well around the point of the ridge and within shouting distance of the Sullivant Hills, he took a casualty count. They had lost Lieutenant Lewiston and the sergeant, and seven of his men had bullet wounds. They made their way back to the beleaguered wood detail.

Major Templeton had found it slow going in the unbroken track of the Westward Trail. No one had used it for weeks, and certainly no one had been through with a horse since the snows. He knew he was running out of time, but there was no quick way to fight the snowdrifts. In some places, the wind had swept the trail clean to the dirt, but in others the snow was piled four feet high.

He had progressed midway past the Lone Pine Ridge, and turned due north where the Westward Trail led through some low hills. He heard rifle fire and

Indian screams ahead to the left. He had been over this trail many times, and knew that his party was still a half mile from the point where he was to close the pincers with Whipple's force.

Before he could do more than curse at his luck, thirty Sioux warriors broke out of a patch of brush and attacked his men. The troopers spread out and returned fire, stopping the Sioux attack in its first rush. There were only three or four rifles among the Sioux, and the hostiles moved away, yet they stayed in harassment range. They made small charges three times at the men, but broke off any serious attack.

Major Templeton knew he was too late for the pincer envelopment. From the distant sound of gunfire, either Whipple had caught the Sioux, or the Indians had attacked Whipple. Major Templeton could do nothing about it. A casualty report showed that none of his men had been hit by the Sioux rifles. He set up a staged withdrawal, leapfrogging two units, with the back one acting as rear guard.

Soon he was out of range of the hostiles and continued at the best possible pace through the snow back to the fort. Once there, he learned that Captain Whipple and his force had not returned.

Colonel Cavanaugh looked at him hard as he tried to explain his actions in the fort commander's office.

"Hell, it was impossible. I've never seen drifts like that on the trail. We tried to go around them, but some of those three-foot-deep drifts were a half mile long. They slowed us almost to a stop in some places.

At last we heard gunfire to the north, around Potlatch Creek, I'd guess. We never got there. About fifty Sioux hit us a half mile from the crossing. We fought them off and beat our way through the drifts back here."

"I'm just glad you didn't have eighty good men, Major. If I remember correctly, you said you could ride through half the Sioux nation with eighty men." Major Templeton looked up sharply, and anger began to build on his face. "Hell, I remember saying that. I meant in dry country in the summer, not in these damn Wyoming snowdrifts. I just hope that Whipple didn't get in trouble up there. He had thirty troopers, some not the most experienced. I just hope to hell he's all right."

"We'll have to wait. He'll probably stay with the woodcutters until they come back. Then we'll know." Colonel Cavanaugh stared at the major for several seconds until the officer's glance came up to meet his superior's.

"Major, did you suffer any casualties?" Cavanaugh asked.

"None, sir. This band of attacking Sioux had maybe three or four rifles. We didn't let them get close enough to use their arrows. My men did well against them."

Cavanaugh nodded. "Maybe now you have a little more respect for the Sioux as fighting men."

"Not a hell of a lot, Colonel. It was the damn snow that beat me, not the Sioux savages."

"Perhaps. Major, I want you on hand to meet

Captain Whipple when he rides in with the timber cutters."

"I'll be there, Colonel. I let those men down, even though it wasn't my fault."

Marcus Cavanaugh dismissed Templeton and settled down behind his desk. His manpower consisted of ten field officers, one surgeon officer, and three hundred and eighty-nine enlisted men, including cooks, farriers, blacksmiths, and clerks. They were scattered in half-filled companies of the 18th Regiment of A, B, E, and G. He had one company of the 2nd Regiment of Cavalry, D Company—or D troop, as he liked to call them.

He considered the cavalry troop. At least half of the men had never ridden before they showed up at Fort Keogh. They were as green as the grass their horses foraged on. There had been little time to train them, but Lieutenant Powell had done the best he could. He concentrated on the best riders and used them when there was a need for cavalry in the field. Even so, there were only forty-eight riders in the troop instead of the eighty-five or ninety that could be expected in a full unit.

He was two-thirds undermanned for his mission. In a tough fight, he could call on about a hundred civilians who were contract employees working to finish the fort. These men had been on hand to do the technical construction on Fort Keogh, but troopers had done much of the manual labor, including cutting, fitting, and setting the logs that formed the palisades.

Part of the problem went back to the inception of Fort Keogh. To the army leaders, this was to be a pacification post. The surrounding Indians had agreed to treaties and would be going to reservations. The fighting in the area was supposed to be over.

Under those guidelines, they had sent an expert engineer and construction man, Major Templeton, and a host of civilian employees and contractors—as well as troops to assist where possible. But Fort Keogh did not have fighting soldiers, even though from the very first, the personnel had been attacked, harassed, and murdered by the Sioux.

If their leaders had signed treaties, it was an even bet that the Sioux had no idea to what they were agreeing. If they did know, they signed just to receive the hatchets, knives, and other gifts that the treaty-makers always gave the chiefs after they signed.

These chiefs probably did not even represent the Sioux nation, and had no authority to sign any paper. One band would send the man who knew the most about the White Eyes and was the best talker. He almost never had any authority to bind the Sioux or any other tribe to a treaty. And from the Sioux point of view, the White Eyes had broken every treaty ever signed, anyway.

Major Templeton had found himself waging a continuing war even while his primary mission was to build a stockaded fort. Now Cavanaugh had inherited the problem. His main job was not keeping the little-used Westward Trail open into Montana. That had been virtually impossible since the first logs went up on the fort. The Indians controlled the route, not the military.

His immediate objective involved bringing in enough wood during the next three months so everyone in the fort didn't freeze to death. He was a goddamn woodman!

Sergeant Major Flynn came in with the morning report. There were twelve men on the medical list for everything from a broken rib to smashed testicles. Nobody had frostbite. Not yet.

"Sergeant, what does the fort have as a wood supply for future use? How many days' supply is stacked in the wood yard?"

"I checked records last year and they made a point to be sure to keep a thirty-day supply, Colonel. But lately we've been running a little short of that, due to the colder weather."

"Which means we have to cut more than we are. Change the standing order on the daily wood detail. Make it five wagons instead of four, and increase the cutters to twenty men."

"Yes, sir."

"What time is it, Sergeant?"

"A little after three, sir. The wood detail should be back at about four if they don't have a lot of trouble."

"Thanks. Let me know the minute the lookout spots them coming. I want to know if they are in a column of fours or fighting their way back with a rear guard."

"Yes, sir. I'll notify the lookouts."

He went out, and Colonel Cavanaugh reconsidered his manpower situation. It was serious, but not critical if all they had to do was sit out the winter. However, if General Cooke ordered them to make raids on the Sioux up the Powder River or the Rosebud, they would be at considerable risk. Cavanaugh decided to put an urgent request in the morning dispatch for seven hundred additional men and officers. There were at least that many lolling around Fort Laramie doing virtually nothing. It wouldn't hurt to get in an early scream for more troops. By some fluke he just might get a hundred or two.

He sorted through the dispatches that had come in that morning via a pair of riders from Fort Reno sixty miles to the south. It had taken them four days to make the trip. At least there was nothing in the dispatches ordering any offensive action.

The dispatch riders would be at the fort for two weeks until the next riders came from Fort Reno. Then this pair would return with dispatches. The team that had come in from Fort Reno two weeks earlier were set to leave first thing in the morning. That meant he had to get everything ready by then, including his morning reports, his casualties, the continuing daily fights with the Sioux, and his letter of promotion for Lieutenant Powell. He also had a letter to General Colt Harding, wherever he might be, concerning the Lightning Troop.

Sergeant Major Flynn came in a half hour later.

"Sir, the lookouts have spotted the returning

wagons. The guard force is large, which must mean that Captain Whipple is escorting them in. There seems to be no fighting, and the troops are in columns of four, half in front and half behind the wagons."

"At least that part is good news." He reached for his fur cap and his overcoat, and headed for the main gate.

Half the fort personnel seemed to be there when the gate swung open and the front section of the escort rode in. Captain Whipple led the troops, and quickly the onlookers saw the two bodies draped double over horses. Captain Whipple quietly directed a sergeant to take the troops into the cavalry yard and dismiss them. He turned his mount toward where the fort commander stood. He swung down and saluted.

"Captain Whipple reporting. We lost two men, sir, Lieutenant Lewiston and Sergeant Constantine. Both good men."

"What the hell happened?"

By the time they walked to the headquarters and into the colonel's office, Whipple had told the colonel about the abortive pincer strategy.

"What it all comes down to is bad timing and my having the wrong half of the cavalry. If I'd had more experienced men, they would have stood and fired back at the Sioux charge, and we wouldn't have lost those two men."

"We can learn from the experience," Colonel Cavanaugh told him. "These Sioux are a lot smarter and a lot tougher than some give them credit for."

9

INSTEAD OF SENDING OUT A RESCUE COLUMN EACH DAY, Colonel Cavanaugh decided to beef up the woodcutting detail's guard by deploying twenty-five infantry and twenty-five cavalry. For three days, the Sioux did not attack.

"They know we're there in force and they don't dare show their shiny, red asses!" Major Templeton asserted, after the wood detail had returned to the fort for the sixth day in a row with no attacks by the hostiles.

The snow had melted down, and travel was getting easier, but there were still three-foot drifts deep in the parts of the forest too dense for the sun to reach.

The logs came in. Crews worked half the day sawing them into eighteen-inch chunks and then splitting them into firewood. Gradually they inched ahead to a thirty-one- and then a thirty-two-day supply of wood. The warmer weather helped a little, but the temperature still dipped well below freezing every night.

On the tenth day, Colonel Cavanaugh began to wonder if the Sioux had holed up in their winter camps. He cut back the work force to four wagons, sixteen choppers, and a dozen mounted guards. At approximately ten-thirty that morning, a signal flashed from the heliograph on Sullivant Hills. The Sioux were attacking with a hundred warriors.

This time it was a scramble. Lieutenant Oberholtzer led the relief party of fifty men, half of them mounted, the rest infantry. He received permission to lead out with the cavalry, leaving Lieutenant Ihander to follow with the troops. The cavalry would be at the scene in thirty minutes. It would take the walking troops an hour to make the three miles.

"Splitting his force," Major Templeton growled as the men left.

"This way the relief column should get there before the wood party is wiped out," Colonel Cavanaugh rasped. "That seems a timely consideration."

Lieutenant Oberholtzer had the best of the cavalry behind him as he cantered, trotted, and cantered again over the well-worn trail, keeping his troops two abreast to take advantage of the beaten track. He pushed the horses, knowing the trip was only three miles. They were within sight of the wagons in twenty-four minutes by Oberholtzer's watch, and he ordered the attack bugle call sounded. The cavalry guard that had accompanied the woodcutters were inside the encircled wagons. The soldiers fired at several dozen attacking Indians, using the logs which had been loaded on the wagons as cover.

"Charge!" Lieutenant Oberholtzer bellowed. His men tramped through the snow directly at the hostiles. The first volley dislodged a dozen Sioux, who charged away to the north along the edge of the hills. The twelve cavalry men inside the circle of wagons mounted and joined the pursuit.

The hostiles edged away from the confrontation more reluctantly this time, fighting from tree to tree. They fell back toward the trail over the ridge. Three troopers pounded around a pair of pine trees and charged three Sioux who seemed unsure of their direction. One produced a rifle and fired. The middle cavalryman screamed and flew out of his saddle. The other two troopers fired and knocked down one of the mounted Sioux. The injured hostile ran, and was hoisted onto another Sioux's mount. They vanished into the denser woods.

"Push them back up the trail!" Oberholtzer bellowed. His voice was all but lost in a volley of rifle fire. Giving chase, the troopers quickly forced the remaining Sioux to race for the trail over Lone Pine Ridge.

Twenty minutes later, Lieutenant Ihander and the infantry arrived. He and Lieutenant Oberholtzer sat on their mounts near the top of the trail and looked down the far side. They could see the Westward Trail below, and Potlatch Creek to the north. Six hostiles moved slowly down the trail less than a hundred yards away. One seemed to be shot, and another held his arm. A third slumped over the neck of his mount.

"Let's charge down there and finish off those three!" Lieutenant Ihander said.

Oberholtzer looked at the terrain. This was the spot the brass had had their big argument about. The situation and the terrain. There were a thousand places in that quarter mile where hostiles could hide.

They could put a hundred mounted men in there and five hundred on foot, and nobody up on the ridge could tell.

"What about it?" Ihander prodded.

"Hell, no, not me. Standing order. On no account chase the hostiles beyond the Lone Pine Ridge trail. This is it, buddy. We go no farther. Let's get our troops back to the woodlot and see how many casualties we have. I think I saw one trooper killed. We'd better check."

They pulled back slowly, keeping a sharp lookout to the rear. Once one of the men fired twice, thinking he saw a hostile. They returned to the woodlot and deployed in a defensive alignment facing the Sullivant Hills. The woodcutters were hard at work filling the four wagons with logs so they could get back to the safety of the fort.

A casualty count revealed three wounded—one seriously—and one dead. The corpse lay facedown over his saddle, his hands and feet tied together with rawhide under the horse's belly. The horse snorted and reared from the smell of death at first, but quieted down.

The troopers finished cutting and loading the logs in record time, and headed back toward the fort. Oberholtzer left three men trailing the party as a rear guard and sent three ahead as scouts. He split the remaining cavalrymen in front and behind the wagons.

They came into the fort and Lieutenant Oberholtzer went directly to Cavanaugh's office to make his report.

"They hit us on the way up, sir, then vanished over the top. We saw three or four stragglers. They were part-way down and not moving very fast. Looked like two or three of them were wounded."

"But you didn't go after them?" Colonel Cavanaugh pressed.

"No, sir. I remembered the standing order. It didn't look like a good bet to me. We hauled our asses out of there and went back to protect the choppers." "Good work, Oberholtzer. I'm sorry about the man who was killed. Consult eyewitnesses, write up a report on it, and send a letter to his next of kin." "Yes, sir."

"That's all, Oberholtzer. Well done."

The lieutenant saluted and left the room.

That night four men sat at a poker game in Major Templeton's quarters. Each man had six bottles of beer lined up beside his place. The poker was the least important part of the evening. Around the table were Major Templeton, Captain Whipple, First Lieutenant Nate Brown and Second Lieutenant Matt Colgan.

"What the hell can we do?" Captain Whipple asked. "Not a hell of a lot we can do right now," Major Templeton growled. "Dammit, we can slow down, or we can function at the expected level but not volunteer to do any special duty not ordered. But I don't even see how that's going to make much difference." "Cavanaugh actually threatened to send you back to Omaha with an uncooperative and disruptive note on your record?" Nate Brown asked.

"Hell, yes. He also threatened to court martial me for insubordination. The bastard could pick his own court and make the charges stick. I'd be out of uniform in a month. There isn't an appeal that does much good unless you're field grade."

They dealt a poker hand of five card draw and played it out.

"I still don't like that standing order about not going down the other side of the ridge," Lieutenant Colgan said. "Hell, we could catch half a dozen of the laggards every time and thin out their ranks. I heard Oberholtzer let three wounded hostiles get away because they were down the other side of the ridge." "Damn, after a few times they'll realize that they're safe once they get over the hump," Brown said. "That means they'll fight harder up to that point, then vanish knowing we haven't ever chased them that far. These savages ain't dumb."

They talked and drank. At about ten that evening, the beer was gone and they started work on a full fifth of Scotch whiskey. An hour later they were still talking army tactics and strategy. The liquor had loosened tongues.

"Major, if you were still running Fort Templeton, what the hell would you be doing about these damn savages and our wood detail about now?" Lieutenant Colgan asked.

Templeton grinned with pleasure at hearing the fort's old name. He tipped his glass of Scotch and drank. Then he smacked his lips.

"What the hell would I do? Hell, that's easy. I'd fix me up a fighting team of about a hundred and fifty of the best troopers we've got. I'd take off after one of them raids on the wood detail and

I'd just keep right on tracking and humping them goddammed Sioux until I made them stand and fight."

He put his glass down and filled it again. "If they didn't fight, I'd hunt them all the way to their winter camp and I'd burn it up, tear it down, smash everything, and destroy their food so they could damn well starve. That's the first damn thing I'd do if I was running this man's army fort."

The three men raised their glasses.

"To the goddamned best fort commander in the whole bloody U.S. Army!" Captain Whipple shouted. They all drank to that.

"Best fort builder and fort commander in all the bastard armies of the whole damn world!" Lieutenant Brown said. They toasted that as well.

The men turned to Colgan. "Best of the best," he said. They laughed and toasted a third time.

Their anger boiled out of them. It was a good way to let off steam, but they weren't ready to go home yet.

"Hey, I ever tell you about my old dad?" Captain Whipple demanded.

The others shook their heads sagely.

"Well, you see my pa lived to be ninety-four. I was a late-life child. Pa was a lively old bastard and one day after my ma dies, he brings home from town this slip of a girl. She was nineteen, she told us. She had the biggest tits I've ever seen, I mean huge. Pa said he was gonna marry her the next day.

"Hell, my brothers and I were concerned. We got Pa off to one side and said, Look, Pa, you're ninety and she's just nineteen and she's gonna want to have sex right there on the old mattress. Age-wise there's a tremendous difference. There could be physical dangers. You should think about this carefully. Pa scrunched up his mouth, closed his eyes, wrinkled his forehead, and nodded. He looked at us and thanked us. Then he told us his decision. Hell, boys, he said, I know it's dangerous, but we're gonna go right ahead and have sex anyway. If the girl dies, she dies!"

The four men burst out laughing. It started a round of story telling, each one more outlandish than the one before.

It was nearly two in the morning when they started singing. At two-thirty the major's wife came in with a broom and began sweeping them out the door. She did it politely, but firmly. As soon as she got to the lamp, she turned down the wick and blew it out.

In the darkness, Major Sawyer Templeton burped loudly. "Hell, men, I guess the party's over."

Saturday was a light duty day. There would be no wood detail. The weather had warmed up and they had thirty-six days' supply of wood. Most of the troops lazed around the barracks, with only essential troops on guard duty, cooking, and other minor chores.

Nate Brown invited Matt Colgan over for some chess that Saturday afternoon. Both had slept in late after the party and neither was totally involved in the game.

"Dammit, Matt, there has to be a way to get Cavanaugh out of his spot as commander of the fort."

Matt laughed. "Sure, there is, but I'd be shot by a firing squad for murder. I don't see any way other than that."

"We're just not thinking hard enough."

Nate's wife came into the room with a fresh pot of coffee and poured a cup for her husband. The dress she wore was tight and the bodice plainly showed the swell of her breasts and a line of cleavage between them.

Matt stared. Linda bent over toward him and poured his coffee. He couldn't move his gaze from the delicious mounds that swung into view. Linda leaned down a little more until her nipples showed, then eased upward and glanced at her husband.

"You owe me five dollars," she said with a small laugh. Nate snorted. "Hell, how could any man resist?"

Matt frowned. "What's this? Some kind of game? Tell me what's going on."

"Yeah, a game. Linda bet me that she could get you staring at her big tits. You stared, all right. You did everything but jump right down her cleavage and waggle your face back and forth."

"Hell, no man will pass up a free gawk at a beautiful pair like those. Damn, but you're a lucky man, Brown."

Nate Brown sat up on his chair. "What did you say, Matt?"

"I said you were a lucky man."

"No, no, before that."

"I said no man will pass up a free look at a beautiful pair of breasts."

Brown snapped his fingers. "We just might have something here."

"What?"

"No man can pass up a free look at a beautiful girl. What about a naked beautiful girl?"

"Sure, if it's free. I don't follow you."

"I think Linda is starting to. I've told her about Cavanaugh, how pristine pure he is. We were talking about getting something on him, something big enough to make him ask for a transfer or face a court martial, right?"

Matt frowned. "Nate, you're not thinking of having Linda ..."

Linda stood there staring from one to the other. At last she grinned. "You might first ask Linda if she would go along with such a plan. She might not want to."

Nate stood, took his wife in his arms, and kissed her long and deep. She clung to him.

"Linda, sweetheart, there's a small favor I want to ask you to do for us, for the good of the post, for the good of the army. All it amounts to is playing a little joke on our esteemed fort commander."

Linda blinked several times and smiled coyly.

"I want you to ask the post commander over here and when he comes in you'll come out of the bedroom almost naked with a torn petticoat on and nothing else. And just about that time I and Matt and Major Templeton and another officer or two will arrive to give you a surprise birthday party. Fancy us finding you just after the colonel has ripped your clothes off!" Linda grinned and kissed her husband. Matt Colgan sat there, grinning and embarrassed.

"Would I do that? Sure. I don't mind men seeing me naked. It kind of excites me, you know what I'm talking about?"

"Of course, Linda, sweetheart. Now why don't you make those cookies you promised? We'll talk about our little trick on the colonel later. Of course, don't say a word about this to anyone."

Linda put her finger across her lips, smiled, and carried the coffee pot back to the kitchen.

Matt stared at Nate Brown. "You're joking. Your wife would do that?"

"You just heard her. She's frank and open about sex."

Matt laughed to hide some of his embarrassment.

"Okay, say that she would do it and we could suddenly have six or seven officers rush into the room and find them both in a compromising situation. How the hell can we court martial our own commanding officer?"

"Hell, I don't know," Brown said. "I'm just a first lieutenant. But I'd bet you a ten dollar bill that Major Templeton can tell us how to do it. Maybe relieve him of his command, put him under house arrest, then hold the court martial. Something like that."

Matt shook his head and laughed again. "Goddamn you, Brown, for a minute there I thought you were serious. This is just a big joke you and Linda thought up to play on me, right?"

"Wrong, Colgan, dead wrong. This is it. This is the idea we've all been straining our pea brains trying to come up with. Come on, let's go see the major right now."

They went down the row of quarters to the major's digs and knocked. Templeton let them in. His eyes were bloodshot, and he squinted at them through the bright sunlight.

"How the hell can you guys look so good already? Damn, it's got to be your youth. What do you want? I'm ready for another nap."

"Major, we've got the method we can use to get your command back here at Fort Templeton."

Nate explained the plan and Templeton went from surprise to enthusiasm in a matter of minutes.

"Damn right it would work! We'll include as witnesses to the show all the officers who have been on his side, like Powell and Oberholtzer. Yes, there are regulations for this. The next highest-ranking officer officially relieves the miscreant and confines him if necessary. Then he brings charges, holds a court martial, and forwards the results to Division head-quarters."

The three men looked at each other. They burst out laughing.

"Hell, I think we might have something," Templeton said. He sobered. "But if something goes wrong, we're putting our army careers in deep shit. We'd be court martialed ourselves, booted out of the army, and might even get some prison time."

"Damn, it's worth the risk," Lieutenant Brown said. "Only I don't see how there can be much risk."

"One problem as I see it," the major said. "What if we come right up to it and your lovely wife won't take off her clothes, Nate? What the hell then?"

Lieutenant Brown chuckled. "Major, you just don't know my wife very well. Come on down to my place right now for a little demonstration."

"What kind of a demonstration?" Templeton asked.

"You'll see, Major, and it will erase any doubts from your mind. I guarantee it."

Major Templeton looked at Colgan. The lieutenant shrugged. Five minutes later they took off their over-coats in the Brown quarters.

Lieutenant Brown told the other two to wait in the living room. His wife was in the small kitchen. He talked to her for a few minutes and went back into the living room.

"Gentlemen, you wanted proof that Linda would be able to do as we wanted when the colonel comes into our quarters. Here's a small demonstration." Linda Brown walked in and said hello to the two men, then went across the room to the bedroom. She wore the same print housedress she had on before. She closed the bedroom door and the men waited. A moment later she stepped out. Her hair was messed up and the front of her dress had been unbuttoned.

She smiled, grabbed the dress, and lifted it off over her head. Then she laughed softly and pulled the white chemise off, exposing her large breasts. For a moment she hesitated, enjoying their widening eyes. Then she slid down the two half-slips she wore, dropping them to the floor. Now she had on only frilly, lacy panties. She stared straight at Major Templeton, pulled the panties off, and threw them at him. The major caught them with a broad smile.

For a moment she looked frightened. Then she began to cry, tears flowing down her cheeks. A minute later she stopped, smiled almost shyly, and gathered up her clothes.

"I used to do some acting in Chicago before I married Nate, Major Templeton. Do you think I can do this part or not?"

Templeton laughed. "Linda, my dear, you're perfect. When this happens, your husband is going to be a captain before he knows it."

10

IN THE TIPI OF WHITE EAGLE, THE SIX LEADING WAR chiefs made final plans for the big fight with the pony soldiers. The warriors would leave in two days and ride to the temporary war camp five miles from the place where the White Eyes cut down the trees.

"I saw a large owl this morning just after daylight," White Eagle said. "That means we should have a handful of days of good weather."

"How many warriors should we take?" Running Bear of the Brule Sioux asked.

"Every warrior we have, leaving the old men and young boys to defend the camps. We will strike the White Eyes with nearly two thousand men and crush them like beetles under our heels."

"Will we take our women along to do the cooking?" Gray Fox of the Sans Arcs Sioux asked. "How long will we be gone in the snow?"

"Eight days at the most, five at the least, Gray Fox. Two days travel each way, then four days to lure the White Eyes into our trap."

Messengers were sent to each of the camps up and down the Powder River. Warriors honed their straightest arrows. Women fixed food, supplies of pemmican and jerky. Temporary lean-tos would be made in the war camp. Buffalo robes would be worn, with a spare one for sleeping carried on each warrior's back.

In White Eagle's tent, Many Skies looked up from her work on a new pair of moccasins for him. Her husband stared at the warming fire. His weapons were ready, and his two war ponies had been fed extra bundles of dry grass he had gathered from under the trees. He would take two mounts, riding the big strong one for the trip through the snow. His favorite war pony, who responded to the slightest touch of his knees, feet, or thighs, would trail behind. In this way his war pony would be fresh for the fight, and he would not risk him slipping and breaking a leg on the snow-covered trail.

White Eagle put on his traveling moccasins. They were twice as heavy as the usual ones, coming halfway up his legs, where they were tied tightly under his leggings. His feet would stay warm inside them. He put on a heavy buckskin shirt and a short buffalo robe, and went outside. The weather was warming, and the creek was not frozen.

White Eagle walked into the woods away from the tipis. Three long arrow shots into the forest he leaned against a large pine tree, closed his eyes, and talked with his cousin, the Snow. For a long time the Snow said nothing. Then the words came.

Your cousin, the Snow, will not hamper you in your great battle with the White Eyes.

White Eagle nodded and thanked the Snow. He opened his eyes and walked again until he was in a place no Sioux had been for many moons—a virgin patch of large pine trees that reached the sky. He looked up and said a small prayer. He watched the towering giants and heard the words come.

Your cousins, the tall pines, will help you in your battle with the White Eyes. We will shelter and protect you.

White Eagle smiled and walked slowly back to his tipi. It was good to read the signs before venturing out on a battle or a raid. This time it was especially important, for now he could tell the combined forces of all the Sioux that the spirits were with them.

That night he stripped naked and lay on his prayer rock, which had an inch of ice covering it. He was not cold as he lay facedown on the ice crust. A half-hour later he groaned and stood up. There had been no sign, no vision, no words from the great spirit.

He walked around his lodge twice. Neither time did he hear a night hawk. He smiled and went back inside. Twice he cast a handful of small twigs into the warming fire. The twigs flamed up, but little smoke rose. The third time he included some wet twigs and a small branch from a green pine bough. This time the twigs flamed and a good quantity of smoke rose. He stood as it drifted toward the opening in the ceiling, studying it, but the spirits did not speak to him through the smoke.

Satisfied, he put two logs on the warming fire and stretched out beside Many Skies. That night he would not lie with any of his three wives, but begin two days of abstinence instead. Many Skies did not touch him, aware of the taboo. She shifted the buffalo robe over him and he dropped off to sleep almost at once.

The next morning White Eagle began his final cleansing. He had an elaborate ritual he went through before a fight or a raid. The purification kept him safe from the White Eyes' bullets. As soon as White Eagle arose, he put on his headdress. It contained only three eagle feathers, and a small medicine bag sewn tightly shut by Many Skies. The soft doeskin of the headdress had been chewed until it was as soft as morning dew. The back part of it had been worked with beads to show the three major spirits: Wind, Fire, and Water.

With the headpiece in place, he left the tipi without eating or drinking. He ran down through the tipis for twenty long arrow shots. Then he turned and, without resting, ran back. He spoke to no one, did not look anyone in the eye, and returned to his tipi panting and tired.

Inside, White Eagle walked around the fire three

times before he sat down. Then he took puffs of dande-lion seeds that he had gathered in a small pouch last summer and saved. He tossed the floating seeds in all four directions over the fire and watched as some sailed upward with the smoke and out the vent of the tipi. Others floated to the side and settled into the ashes or the area around the fire. More of the seeds went out the smoke hole than fell to the ground. It was a good sign.

Now White Eagle went to the small parfleche made of dried rawhide. He opened it with great respect, and took out the band's medicine bundle. Several items were rolled up in a piece of decorated doeskin. On top of a woven mat made of soft marsh grasses lay the scared objects of the tribe. One was the dried head and shoulders of a hawk with the tail feathers fastened to it, tied securely with sinew. White Eagle drew it out slowly, with great emotion, praying each instant that it would be whole. It was. The Hawk symbolized a warrior's bravery in battle.

Next to it was a White Eye's scalp with dark, braided hair. The scalp was fastened to a piece of beaded buffalo hide that could be worn around the neck of a worthy chief.

He stared at the scalp and hair for a long time. He prayed that he and his warriors would take many scalps to make the spirits happy, and that the sacred buffalo would soon return to the ranges. Below that lay the sacred eagle claw. The leg bone had been carefully cleaned of flesh and wrapped with buckskin to form a handle. Feathers around the base of the claw had been retained, and the claw glistened a stark white and gray.

This icon was the personal treasure of White Eagle. The eagle claw was to help the leaders of the band be sharp and prudent in their planning of raids and battles. Below the eagle claw lay a buffalo horn. It had been broken off in a great battle many moons ago by a great warrior in the band; although the buffalo had killed the warrior, he had wounded it so grievously that the animal soon died as well. The band took the broken horn as a symbol of the Ogalala's power over the buffalo and the importance of the beast to their survival.

It was nearly midday when White Eagle had finished his prayers to each of the artifacts in the medicine bag. He rolled them back up, and put the bundle in the parfleche. He carried it outside to the center of the gathered tipis and called out to all in a loud voice. The most holy of all the sacred rituals would be performed that day—the viewing of the medicine bundle by full-fledged Ogalala Sioux warriors.

White Eagle put the bundle on a stump and slowly unrolled it. He exposed one item and eighty warriors formed a line. Each one prayed at the medicine bundle for as long as he wished. It was well after sundown when the ritual was completed. The warriors had stood in a small group after they prayed, but did not speak until the last warrior had finished. They raised their hands over their heads in a salute, and each went directly to his own tipi.

White Eagle went back to his tipi from the ceremonial stump. He put the medicine bundle with his other treasured possessions. Then he left at once and walked through the snow to his praying rock. He stripped naked and lay on the rock facedown.

The ice felt cold. He lay there for five minutes, feeling great pain. His feet and hands and the side of his face were numb. He pushed all thoughts of the fight ahead from his mind and concentrated. He thought of the past and the times when he had talked with the great spirit, and accepted his will. The cold receded and his body warmed. The rock became his friend. He opened his soul to listen for the words of the spirit.

It was another half-hour before he heard anything. Then an owl hooted in the far-off brush. He heard the cry of a night bird nearby, and the answer of its mate. Then all was quiet. The first murmurings came softly. He listened harder. The voices came in a confusing jumble, then stopped. One voice emerged.

He saw a spirit in the shape of a mountain lion. It roared and clawed the air, then turned directly toward him. The creature seemed only a few inches away from his face. White Eagle could smell the animal's breath; he could see the glint in its eyes. Then the form wavered. When it cleared, he saw an ancient Sioux warrior with deep lines in his face wearing war paint, with a bone hanging from one ear.

It was One Ear, the fabled warrior of six generations ago, the most revered and honored of the old chiefs, who was remembered in song and dance. The warrior spoke.

"White Eagle, you go to fight the White Eyes. It is good. Fight long and hard, fight for the honor of the Ogalala Sioux. Let no water or food pass your lips during the day of the fighting. You will bring glory to our people."

There were questions he wanted to ask, but White Eagle could not move his lips. The face of the great chief, the greatest warrior of the Ogalala, faded. In its place came the snarling head of the mountain lion. Its tail flicked back and forth, as if it were about to strike. The great cat crouched on its strong legs. In one terrible second, it leaped through the air at White Eagle's head.

The great chief did not flinch. He waited for the jaws and the sharp teeth to sink into his flesh. Just before the mountain lion reached him, it vanished.

White Eagle stood. His back was cold, yet his bare stomach, which had been pressed against the ice on the rock, was warm. He dressed and walked back to his tipi. His cleansing for the great battle was complete. He had seen the great man himself, Chief One Ear, and he had talked with him. The chief was proud, and gave his blessing. White Eagle was ready for the fight.

The next morning, the move began. Hundreds of warriors rode along the trail beside the Powder River, working upstream to the south—toward the White Eyes.

The warriors in each band stayed together. By the

time they passed the last camps of the Sans Arcs, they numbered nearly two thousand. There was still a foot of snow on the ground. But White Eagle had heard the owl. He was sure there would be no new snow for four days.

The braves moved slowly, prepared for a two-day ride to get to the war camp. Befitting his position, White Eagle and his Ogalalas led the warriors. Behind them, the men were strung out in a rag-tag, unorganized formation for more than half a mile. In some places, the riders went single file. Sometimes there would be ten abreast, yelling, talking, and teasing each other with nervous energy.

At the end of the first day, White Eagle determined that they had covered more than half the distance. They slept among a thick stand of pine and cottonwood, and rose early with the sun. They arrived at the war camp two hours before sunset, where they met the war parties which had been harassing the soldiers at the pinery for weeks.

A large, double lean-to had been built for their arrival. It was ten feet high and sloped down so there was a twenty-foot spread between the poles. It was twenty feet long and had been covered with pine boughs. It would not keep the rain out, but any new snow would accumulate on the roof and freeze into a water-tight seal.

Under it, two Fire pits glowed warmly with coals. It would be Chief White Eagle's lodge for the time they spent at the war camp. The other warriors set about building small lean-tos; by darkness, everyone had shelter. White Eagle took reports from the men who had been on the scene. One warrior, Little Neck, was the spokesman.

"We have been raiding their wood parties, hurting them where we can. Each time we attack, they send men on horseback and we must fall back. We do as we have been told, but so far they have not been lured into the trap down the far side of the Ridge of Many Snows. For several days, they sent a large force to guard the woodcutters. On these days we did not attack. But the day they sent a small force, we attacked again, and the rescue force followed us. They did not fall for our bait of 'wounded' warriors who had lagged behind the main party. We were in position for the ambush, but they did not come into our trap."

"How many pony soldiers do they send against you?"

"Three hands of woodcutters and four hands of guards. Then the alarm is given, and many more soldiers rush to rescue the wood people."

"Then we'll have to send out a larger force to hit their woodcutters," White Eagle reasoned. "They will need to send more men to rescue them."

He looked around. Most of the other chiefs were there, and he saw them nodding in agreement.

"Little Neck, tomorrow we will attack the wood haulers. You will be at my right hand to show me where to go and where you have set the ambushes. We will work together. We will lead two hundred warriors in the first attack and overwhelm the woodcutters if we can. When more pony soldiers come, we will challenge them if they do not fall into our trap. We will meet them and cut them into pieces and take many scalps."

That night White Eagle found a new prayer rock and spent an hour in prayer and serenity. The spirits did not speak.

In the morning, he chose forty men from each of the five tribes and led them to Potlatch Creek. The remainder of the warriors rode behind them. They would stay in the thick woods near Potlatch Creek to spring the trap.

Chief Running Bear took five hundred warriors and hid them in the crags and gullies on the trail that led across the Ridge of Many Snows. Another ambush was set by Gray Fox of the Sans Arcs, who hid his braves on each side of the great trail northwest. Dense brush and pine trees gave perfect cover for an ambush.

After setting the traps and forming the initial attack group, there were still fifteen hundred Sioux waiting to charge the White Eyes wherever they found them. They waited north of Potlatch Creek in heavy timber, sure that every man would count coup before the sun set.

White Eagle and his band of two hundred warriors swept around the far end of the Ridge of Many Snows and angled toward five low hills. He knew the area well. They waited before scouting out the woodcutters.

White Eagle felt the thrill of approaching battle.

This was what he was born for. He was an Ogalala Sioux warrior, feared by his enemies, respected by other chiefs, and loved by his three wives. Even the spirits were with him in this fight. He rode with a look of anticipation on his rugged, copper face.

11

At Fort Keogh, the day dawned cold and cloudy. Colonel Cavanaugh watched the clouds as he hurried through the freezing weather toward his office. It would not snow that day, he decided. There was no wind, and it was too cold.

He stomped into the office, kicked the snow off his boots on the braided rug, and checked in with Sergeant Major Flynn.

"Anything earth-shattering yet, Flynn?"

"Sir, that Indian scout you said you wanted to see is waiting right over there."

The sergeant major nodded toward a man standing near the pot-bellied stove in the center of the room. He was tall for an Indian, five-six or seven. His hair had been cut short, and he wore blue army pants and issue boots topped by a heavy buckskin jacket with fringes. He looked at Colonel Cavanaugh and came to attention.

"Sir! I have much news."

Cavanaugh nodded and turned back to Sergeant Major Flynn. "This is Kahnachee, the Arapaho who came in last night from the north, right?"

"Yes, sir, that's what he told me. We bunked him down in the stables and fed him. He's itching to tell you something, sir."

"Give me about five minutes to look over my desk and then bring in Kahnachee."

The fort commander went into his office and turned to the large scale map on the wall. It showed most of the Dakota Territory. There was part of the territory of Montana up at the top.

Fort Keogh was in the upper quarter of Wyoming. The nearest outposts were Fort F. C. Smith, just over the line in Montana, and Fort Reno in the south. It was a lot of country, especially when it was full of Sioux warriors.

A knock sounded on the door and Sergeant Major Flynn poked his head in. "Kahnachee to see you, sir." Colonel Cavanaugh turned from the map and appraised the Indian again. He could be a half-breed. His features were slightly more refined than many Indians. He went to his desk and waved the Indian to a seat across from him.

"Now, Kahnachee, you said you had something you wanted to tell me."

"Yes, Colonel, sir. I am a scout. Work for bird colonel at Fort Reno two year. Very good English. No Indian., scouts here?"

"No, I'm afraid not, Kahnachee. We don't have any money to hire any. I'm working on that."

"Kahnachee come from north. Hear many things.

See many things. Scout usual pay, two dollar a day. For you, Kahnachee work for one dollar a day." "How could you help me as a scout, Kahnachee?" "Tell you about Indians in north, along Rosebud, along Powder River. Many Indians."

"And if I hire you, you will tell me about this?" Colonel Cavanaugh laughed. "Kahnachee, you must be part Irish. You see, I know there are Indians along the Rosebud and the Powder. Almost every day fifty to a hundred Sioux hit our wood-gathering detail about three miles from here."

"Only few Indians there." The scout stopped. Cavanaugh shrugged and dug a dollar bill from his pocket and handed it to the Arapaho. "Tell you what, I'll hire you for one day. You tell me what you think is happening and if I find something new, and you're right, I'll hire you for a month on trial. OK?"

"Fine, fine." Kahnachee nodded. "So many Sioux on Powder, not just usual winter bands like five or six. All bands from this part of country camp end to end along Powder for maybe fifteen miles."

"Fifteen miles of tipis? Sitting there in the snow? The Sioux don't hold big councils in the winter, Kahnachee."

"Kahnachee see with own eyes. Maybe two thousand tipis along Powder River."

Cavanaugh frowned. He got up and went over to

the big map. "Show me, Kahnachee. Where are there two thousand tipis on the Powder?"

The Indian moved to the map with quick, smooth steps.

"We're here, at Fort Keogh." Cavanaugh showed him where the fort was, and traced his finger along the rivers. "The Powder starts up behind us in the Big Sandy and runs north to the Yellowstone, which runs farther north into the Missouri. Where were the Sioux?"

Kahnachee followed the map from one tributary to the next until he came to the Powder River, more than fifty miles from the fort. He pointed along that stretch of the Powder that flowed fifteen miles north and on into Montana.

"Two thousand, you say. There aren't that many Ogalalas and Brules put together."

"No. But also there the Sans Arcs, Unkpapas, and Miniconjous. All the Sioux nation."

"A big gathering, a council? Now, in the middle of winter? Why, Kahnachee?"

"I hear all Sioux join together for two big fights. One here at Fort Keogh. Next big fight at Fort Smith much north here."

Captain Cavanaugh went back to his seat. Something was unsettling about this. If it were true, it could mean more than just harassment of the wood details. They didn't need two thousand warriors to keep up their attacks on the wood train.

"All right, Kahnachee, it is possible. How did you find out all this?"

"I am Indian. I listen. Others talk. It is not so hard."

Colonel Cavanaugh went to his door and rapped sharply twice. Sergeant Major Flynn came through seconds later.

"Put up this army scout for the next week. He's on the payroll now. Any word on the woodcutters yet?" "Too early, sir. They've little more than sharpened their axes by this time. Another hour will tell." "Keep me informed."

The sergeant and the scout went out the door, while Colonel Cavanaugh paced back to the map and stared at it. With a pencil, he made a light circle around the area to which the scout had pointed. It was roughly ten miles from the Montana border.

If what Kahnachee had said was true, there could be thousands of hostile Sioux warriors headed for Fort Keogh. His men could make a fight out of it if they all were inside the fort. He thought at once about ammunition supply. It was not the best. With their rapid fire, the new Henry and Spencer rifles ate up ammunition at a fantastic rate. A good man with a Spencer could get off seven rounds in less than nine seconds. A good man with a breechloader could fire three rounds in nine seconds.

Cavanaugh had been aware of how boxed in he was at Fort Keogh. He had no intelligence at all except his heliograph on Sullivant and Pilot hills, neither of them more than three miles from the fort. He didn't send patrols out in each direction to keep track of Indian activities. If he tried it, he'd lose whole patrols every other trip. He didn't know what was out there only fifty miles away.

Sergeant Major Flynn knocked, and then opened his door.

"Sir, there was a break in the clouds long enough for them to send a message from the heliograph on Sullivant Hills. The Sioux have attacked again. This time they have at least two hundred mounted warriors. It looks like the wood crew will be overrun for certain."

"Sergeant Major, order out seventy-five men; we'll have to respond in force. Half cavalry. Captain Whipple wanted the next assignment. Move it, Flynn!"

Captain Whipple came on a run from his company. "I'll take the command out, Colonel."

"You've got it. Take seventy-five men. Half infantry. Units are being alerted now."

"I want Lieutenant Powell with me on the cavalry."
"Fine, tell him. We've got to move fast or there might not be any point in going at all. Get the cavalry out fast and relieve the woodcutters before they are over-whelmed."

"Yes, sir." Captain Whipple turned and ran for the barracks. Five minutes later the troops were assembled, with a few of the cavalrymen still straggling into formation. There were seventy-seven men and two officers. Major Templeton came riding up on his horse, outfitted for battle.

"Colonel, sir. I formally request command of this

rescue column. I appeal to you because of my seniority."

"Do you know two hundred savages have attacked the woodcutters?"

"Yes, sir. I've had more experience in this kind of fighting, sir. Let me have it."

Colonel Cavanaugh paused. He nodded. "Very well, Major, the command is yours."

"I want to take Captain Whipple rather than Powell. I work closer with Whipple."

"Very well. Get them moving."

Lieutenant Powell sat on his horse near Colonel Cavanaugh and watched the troops move into columns. At the last minute, two civilians with Henry repeating rifles rushed up to Major Templeton. He waved them into the column behind him. As the troops rode and marched out of the gate, a final count showed seventy-seven enlisted cavalry and infantry, two civilians, and two officers.

"I'll be damned," Colonel Cavanaugh said to Lieutenant Powell. "Templeton has the eighty men he bragged he needed. Now let's see if he can wade right through two hundred of the warriors of the Sioux nation."

Lieutenant Powell seemed troubled. "Sir, those are the best of my men. I just don't like to see them go into a battle without me to direct them."

"Lieutenant, there will be a lot more Sioux fighting before this winter is over. You'll see your share. This time it's Templeton and Whipple."

White Eagle and his band of two hundred mounted warriors came around the end of the Five Little Hills, and positioned themselves where they could see the Blue Shirts at work cutting down trees. The warriors moved up through the trees, getting as close as they could without being seen.

When the first brave was spotted and a shot came from the guards around the woodcutters, White Eagle lifted his rifle. The warriors rushed at the firewood detail. This was not a harassment—it was a full-scale battle. The Sioux formed in a wedge, with White Eagle leading the point. The enemy rifles fired. Three warriors fell, then four more, but the Sioux swarmed forward.

The six men among the Sioux who had rifles started using them, firing and reloading as they rode. Soon they were in bow-and-arrow range, and a hail of deadly missiles dropped on the woodcutters and their defenders.

White Eagle and his men closed the last hundred yards to the pony soldiers quickly. More warriors fell, and some of the horses went down. But dozens more pushed forward to take their place. White Eagle led the charge over the last few yards and into the middle of the Blue Shirts. None of the soldiers had time to mount a horse and attempt a getaway. They fought with rifles and pistols, hand and fist.

White Eagle used his bow and killed two of the woodcutters as they swung their axes at the war ponies. One soldier killed a warrior with a rifle shot from six feet away, knocking him off his pony. The White Eye soldier grabbed the war pony and leapt on his back, riding away to the south. Two warriors on ponies raced after him, shooting arrows. The third one hit the fleeing White Eye in the back, severed his spinal column, and killed him instantly.

More than half of the soldiers and woodcutters had been killed on the initial charge. It was an easy matter to dispatch the rest of them. White Eagle whirled his war pony back and forth, hunting for new targets.

An older soldier with yellow marks on his sleeve rose up before him and fired his pistol. The war chief's magic was strong, and the bullet missed. White Eagle released his bow. His aim was true. The sergeant drowned in his own blood, a broad-tipped arrow in his throat.

Two minutes after the Sioux launched their attack against the woodcutting detail, every one of the White Eyes lay dead. The scalping began. Every warrior who dealt a death blow had the honor of taking the White Eye's scalp and tying it to his surcingle. A brave from the scouting party posted on one of the Five Little Hills rode up at top speed.

"More pony soldiers left the fort and are coming this way," he reported. "Many White Eyes—eight times both hands."

White Eagle shouted a warning. The warriors had found all of the White Eyes' weapons, and stripped many of the bodies naked, cutting and hacking them. If the White Eyes' spirits were to meet them in the hereafter, the spirits would be crippled and unable to fight well.

The warriors cut the horses and mules from the wood wagons and drove them away. Half of the warriors hurried around the far end of the Five Little Hills to Potlatch Creek. There, they waited for the rescue party from Fort Keogh.

Colonel Cavanaugh and Lieutenant Powell went directly to the blockhouse lookout near the main gate. It was the best view of the pinery where the woodcutters were.

Major Templeton quick-marched his troops while keeping the horses at a slow trot. That way the infantry kept up with the horses as they moved down the wood road. Before they reached the Sullivant Hills, the troop turned right and went along the north side behind the wood road.

"What the hell is he doing?" Lieutenant Powell sputtered.

Cavanaugh lowered his field glasses. "He might be swinging around in back of the hills so he can come around the other end and take the savages from the back. That way he could crush the attacking force between his men and the guards at the circled wagons."

"That's going to take longer. I just hope those thirty-six men out there at the pinery can hold out until he gets there."

Soon the troops vanished behind the hills and from there on they could only speculate on the outcome.

White Eagle and half his force remained near the

pinery, waiting for the rescue party to appear. Many had scalps dangling from lances and surcingle's. Two of the warriors wore the pony soldiers' wide-brimmed hats. One had on a blue shirt with many yellow stripes on the sleeve. White Eagle was pleased. They had captured many rifles and several revolvers, and axes and saws as well.

Soon a scout rode down from the hills. The formation of pony soldiers had swung to the north of the Five Little Hills. The White Eyes had changed their pattern of riding quickly to the defense of the woodcutters.

At once, White Eagle knew the reason: They would come around the far end of the hills in an attempt to attack the Sioux from the rear. It was a good strategy, but he was ready. White Eagle began to move a hundred of his warriors forward.

Major Sawyer Templeton swung his troops along at quick-march down the wood road from the fort. At last, he had a worthwhile command; eighty men and two hundred damned Sioux to challenge, only two and a half miles away.

As he rode, Templeton began to wonder why this sortie had to be like all the others, an inconclusive confrontation in which a few rounds were exchanged and the Sioux were chased off across the ridge where they almost begged the troopers to come down and fight. The Sioux attacked the woodcutters about midway along the Sullivant Hills. Templeton realized that if he swung around the other side of the hills, he could march to the end, turn back to the woodlot, and attack the savages from the rear.

He told his plan quickly to Captain Whipple. The younger officer shouted with delight. They swung the column off the wood road, and moved north of the first low hill in the series of five. The troops muttered, wondering what was happening. Captain Whipple rode back along the line, telling them the strategy and urging them on. Some of them cheered.

Templeton knew that Cavanaugh would be watching him from the palisades of Fort Keogh, and would see the move. In his mind, he thought he would be congratulated for it. He pushed the troops faster, in a hurry to get to the woodlot and rout the savage Sioux.

As the soldiers progressed, Templeton noticed something strange. There had been a good deal of firing from the pinery when they came down the trail, although they had never come close enough to see it. Now it seemed that the firing had all but stopped. It occurred to him that the redskins had pulled back out of range. He smiled, emboldened by his plan. He'd hit the Indians so hard they'd be in their happy hunting ground before noon.

A few moments later, Templeton's men rounded the last of the five hills. He spotted a small force of mounted Sioux ahead and to the left near a long island between the branches of the Big Sandy Creek. Templeton ignored them. He looked to the south and east around the last of the Sullivant Hills.

What he saw surprised and startled him. A force of at least a hundred Sioux warriors were coming toward him, their lances held high. And what was worse—many of them carried rifles.

The Sioux army was in a shallow valley when the Blue Shirts rounded the far hill. The two forces stared at each other from less than fifty yards away. White Eagle spoke to half a dozen warriors, telling them to hold back and lure the White Eyes forward. Then he lifted his rifle and pointed between the two hills. His men galloped through the opening before the pony soldiers could spur after them. The war chief took the lead, bringing his warriors across the creek, up the trail, and over the Ridge of Many Snows.

The six warriors let the soldiers see them, then surged forward out of sight, repeating the action several times. Soon they came to the crest of the ridge. They charged down the far side to a good spot and pushed their horses out of sight in small ravines and brushy spots. There they eagerly lay in wait.

The sound of firing from the woodlot continued to carry to the fort for some time after Templeton marched out. With the sun under widespread cloud cover, there would be no more reports from the helio-graph. With nothing to see, Colonel Cavanaugh and Powell started back to the headquarters building when one of the lookouts reported, "Sir, we've spotted more than twenty mounted hostiles about four hundred yards in the edge of the pine trees in front of the fort."

"Sergeant, fire one spherical case shot from your Howitzer."

"Yes, sir."

The weapon was loaded, set for altitude, and the fuse cut and lighted. The roar of the Howitzer from the blockhouse sent shock waves through the wooden structure and half deafened the men on the platform. Both officers held their hands over their ears.

They watched the case shot streak from the muzzle and explode in the midst of the Sioux horsemen. Those not killed or wounded fled back into the pine trees.

"Good shooting, Sergeant. Have another round ready in case they return. It must have been a scouting expedition to test us." Colonel Cavanaugh remained in the lookout but saw no further signs of Indians. The firing from the pinery had tapered off. That could mean good news or bad.

He summoned surgeon Captain Hirum Hines, and ordered him to move out with an ambulance and medical supplies. Two mules pulled the light ambulance wagon with six mounted men along as an escort. The ambulance left with the mules at a trot and quickly worked its way down the wood road. It soon vanished behind the brow of the nearest hill.

Colonel Cavanaugh paced the lookout and waited. He checked his watch when the doctor left. There had been no more sign of the hostiles in front of the fort. The Gun-That-Shoots-Twice, as the Indians called the exploding cannon shot, had discouraged them in its deadly fashion.

"Twenty-six minutes since the doctor left," Cavanaugh said. "He should be at the woodcutting area."

They heard little gunfire for the moment. What they did hear seemed to be coming from farther north of the woodlot. The sun wove in and out of clouds, but the heliograph operator on the lookout said there wasn't time enough to send a message. He tried twice to ask the Sullivant Hills for a report, but he couldn't find enough sun to do the job. Then the clouds blew over the sun in a solid mass.

Those on the north lookout could see down along Little Sandy Creek for almost two miles to where the wood road vanished behind the hills. Cavanaugh checked his watch again. The doctor had been gone for thirty-five minutes now.

"I wish I knew to God what's happening out there!" the colonel raged. "We should have set up a telegraph wire out to the woodlot for instant communication."

"Colonel, the ambulance is coming back!" one of the lookouts shouted.

Cavanaugh put his glasses on the wagon and saw it racing back along the wood road.

"Powell, take ten cavalry and go meet them. Quickly!"

Five minutes later, the cavalry escort raced from the main gate at a gallop heading down the wood road.

"Why is the doctor coming back?" Colonel Cavanaugh shouted, not expecting an answer. "All six of the escort riders are with him, right?"

"Yes, sir, and the ambulance driver. I don't see the captain."

Lieutenant Powell and the ambulance wagon met about a mile from the fort. The wagon never slowed. Powell rode alongside and evidently talked with the driver or the doctor. Then he left the escort and galloped back toward the fort, leaving the others behind him.

Colonel Cavanaugh went to the main gate to meet Powell. The officer's horse was near exhaustion. Two troopers took the animal; they walked him, wiped him down, and kept' him from foundering. "Sir," Powell said, looking anguished. "Captain Hines says the woodlot train was overrun. All but two were killed by the big attack. Captain Hines has the two wounded who crawled into brush where the Indians didn't find them. The rest of the wood team was killed, mutilated, and hacked to pieces—their horses, mules, weapons, and most of the uniforms all taken."

"Damnit! Why this time? They must have had the men to overrun the woodlot detail at any time."

He looked at the ambulance racing toward the fort from a half mile away. "Can the doctor save the two wounded?"

"He thinks he can. He has more bad news, as well, sir. He said he tried to follow some fighting he heard. He went to the end of the hills and attempted to cross the Big Sandy Valley hoping to link up with Major Templeton. He found the valley swarming with savages. He said there must have been at least five hundred of them. There were also more than a hundred hostiles around the Lone Pine Ridge. Since he didn't find Templeton where he should have been, he says the only conclusion is that Templeton took his men over the ridge after the Sioux."

12

Major Templeton sent the cavalry under Captain Whipple to rout the savages at the far end of the ridge where it turned toward Potlatch Creek.

"Rout those bastards and push them back toward the creek and the Westward Trail. I'll go over the ridge after these warriors ahead of us. I'll meet you down there by the creek and the trail, and we'll smash them between us!"

Captain Whipple called to his men and swung away with thirty-two cavalry and mounted infantrymen. They dashed toward the small band of Sioux north of the small island.

Major Templeton urged the rest of the men to trot forward after the Sioux. Half a dozen stragglers darted through the gap between the hills, disclosing the direction of the warriors' flight. They were running like hell from the cavalry. The six mounted Sioux were trying to get through a narrow place on the upward trail. His men fired eight or ten shots at them, wounding one. Quickly the Indians vanished upward on the trail.

None of the enemy was seen again until Major Templeton and the front elements of his infantry made it to the top of the ridge. He looked down the other side. The trail was icy and snow-covered since it was on the shady side of the slope. Less than a hundred yards below, a wounded Sioux had dismounted and was trying to bind up a leg wound. Templeton lifted his Spencer and fired three times. The savage slithered around some rocks until he was out of sight.

When the balance of his men hit the top of the ridge, Templeton never hesitated. He waved them forward down the slope. In the back of his mind he remembered Cavanaugh's standing orders. This was supposed to be the terrible suicide trail, never to be traversed. The major saw nothing so terrible about it.

He hurried down the grade with his infantrymen until the entire contingent was strung out behind him. He was nearly two-thirds of the way down, disappointed that he hadn't found any more injured or wounded Sioux, and no dead.

A wild Sioux war cry echoed around both sides of the canyon.

Suddenly, from the bottoms of gullies, behind trees and ice-covered boulders, hundreds of Sioux warriors rose up on all sides. With bows and arrows and rifles, they sent a withering hail of cross fire at the helpless U.S. Army troopers.

The soldiers scattered to find cover. Templeton hid

behind a large rock, but at once took fire from the other side of the canyon. He squirmed into an icy shelter between boulders that offered protection on both sides.

"Cut down the sons-of-bitches!" Templeton bellowed to encourage his troops. He saw the trooper just ahead of him take an arrow in the shoulder. The man screamed in pain and stood up, trying to pull the arrow out. Within seconds, six more arrows pierced his body and rendered the trooper immobile.

Templeton watched for a target, found one fifty yards across the canyon, and waited for the savage to lift up and shoot an arrow. Templeton adjusted his aim a fraction of an inch and fired. The big .52 caliber slug tore through the Sioux's chest, blasting a hole in his heart the size of a fist.

"Make every shot count, men!" Templeton screamed. At that moment a force of two hundred more Sioux, mounted on war ponies, stormed up the trail from the bottom of the canyon.

Many of Templeton's men had already used up their standard forty rounds of ammunition, and the extra rounds they had were nowhere near enough. Those who ran out presented a pitiful sight. A private threw his useless rifle at a Sioux, then fired six rounds from his pistol. Two Sioux avoided his rounds and ran toward him, shooting two arrows.

When they captured him, he already had three arrows in his legs and upper chest. Then the torture began. They cut him with knives while he screamed in agony and terror.

Templeton got off one shot at them, drilling a slug through the head of one of the savages. His own ammunition was running low. He watched helplessly, his men being slaughtered. There were close to a thousand Sioux in the small ravine before they stopped pouring in. A brave rose three feet from him. Major Templeton shot him through the chest with his pistol. He reloaded another round to keep six in the cylinder.

Something moved behind him. He swung around and saw three Sioux with arrows drawn in their bows. He fired three times and dove to the side, but couldn't avoid all the arrows. He killed two of the savages and wounded a third. An arrow lodged painfully in his right leg.

He whirled around, his rifle ammunition gone, the weapon useless. He held a knife in one hand, and his pistol in the other. There wasn't even time to reload the revolver. He had three shots left.

Another trooper screamed in agony. Templeton dared not look up. A Sioux ran past without spotting him. Another one looked down at him and drew back his arm to throw a knife. Templeton shot him in the face with his revolver. He looked down the hill where three troopers stood, lifting their arms in a gesture of surrender. Sioux arrows slammed into them and they went down, dead before they hit the ground.

All around men were screaming and dying. A brave held a bloody scalp aloft and gave a war cry. The scalped trooper staggered up off a snow-covered rock, blood streaming down his face, his eye sockets blind, red holes where the savage had gouged out his eyes. The trooper screamed until another Sioux with a ten-foot lance ran him through.

Another Sioux found Major Templeton, and lunged at him with a knife. He slashed at the warrior's throat, severing the carotid artery. Warm Sioux blood sprayed over Major Templeton. The next Sioux shot his bow without aiming. The arrow missed. Major Templeton fired his next-to-last revolver round. It shot upward under the Sioux warrior's chin, and tore off half his scalp when it exited the back of his skull.

Templeton felt his belt but found no more rounds for the Colt .45. He was down to his last bullet. He put the muzzle of the big gun against the side of his head just forward of his ear and leaped to his feet, bellowing wildly.

"You bastards will never take me alive! Cowards, ugly savages!" A dozen Sioux turned their bows toward him. Before he felt the bite of metal arrowheads, Templeton pulled the trigger.

On the other side of the ridge, Captain James Whipple turned his cavalry around and rode at a trot toward the island. The cluster of Sioux had disappeared and there was nothing at the end of the ridge but the two small streams that came together after splitting around the island. Beyond the ridge was Potlatch Creek where it crossed the Westward Trail. If he didn't find the Sioux, he decided to wait there with his cavalry to rendezvous with Major Templeton.

His troops splashed across the creek and rode for the end of the ridge. They saw no hostiles. He led his men forward. Soon he saw Potlatch Creek with a fringe of bare brush and gaunt trees along its icy shore. To the right was a forested slope that rose fifty yards from the creek. The best route was between the slope and the creek.

"Look sharp now, men!" Captain Whipple called. "Could be we drove that small band into these trees. Keep your trigger fingers ready."

Each cavalryman had a pistol and a rifle that could fire seven shots without reloading. They rode past the small hill. All was calm. A bird called somewhere ahead of them.

They were halfway through. Whipple had seen no enemy for ten minutes. The same bird call came from behind them somewhere. Captain Whipple frowned.

Suddenly, rifle Fire exploded from the woods and brush on both sides of them. Three of the troopers went down in the first volley.

"Dismount and take cover behind your horses!" Captain Whipple shouted. The men slipped from their mounts and looked for targets. There were none. Blue gunsmoke came from the brush and trees, but there were no second shots. Most of the Indians couldn't figure out how to fire their looted rifles a second time. A few seconds later the mounted warriors broke from the trees, screeching Sioux war cries and firing arrows.

They charged forward. Confused and shaken, the cavalry was caught in the open in an ambush that rapidly cut their number in half.

Captain Whipple stood behind the neck of his horse and fired his Spencer carbine at a charging Sioux. He hit the redskin in the side, blowing him off the war pony. His next shot missed a savage but struck the pony behind him, killing it and dumping the rider into the snow.

"Move toward the creek and the woods!" Whipple bellowed. Few of the troopers could hear him. One or two tried. As soon as they left the knot of cavalrymen and horses, they were cut down by a volley of arrows.

"Fight them off!" Captain Whipple screeched. He fired again and his Spencer was out of rounds. He drew his revolver.

Three troopers and two horses in front of Whipple went down in a thrashing, screaming, death struggle, exposing him. A pair of Sioux warriors rode hard directly at him, shooting arrows. The first hit his horse in the neck. Another whispered past his face.

The second Sioux carried a long lance with a steel tip. They were on him before he realized it. The lance drove into Captain Whipple's horse. The animal brayed, and slumped down on its front knees. Whipple barely leaped away before it rolled on its side, breaking the lance and killing itself in the same instant.

Captain Whipple dashed backwards on foot toward the other troopers and horses. There had been thirty-two of them, and now there were less than half that number.

"Men, run for the brush. Use your horses as shields. Let's all go, now!"

The Sioux screamed in defiance and raced in to cut them off. The distance was short, and the soldiers reached their goal. They abandoned their horses and settled behind the first good-sized trees they could find for protection.

"How many here?" Captain Whipple called. Six men shouted out their last names. "How are we on ammunition? I'm down to my pistol and about ten rounds."

Nobody had over twenty rounds. They had three Spencer carbines left, and each man had a pistol.

"Here they come!" one man shouted.

Twenty Sioux, riding their war ponies, crashed into the brush directly ahead of them.

Captain Whipple fired once as one brave surged past. The revolver round hit the hostile in the back of the head and drove him off the war pony. He heard one of his men scream, ending in a blubber and silence.

When the rush of the twenty savages was past, Whipple called for a count. Only four men answered. He looked around and realized the Sioux's sweep had also chased away the four horses the group had managed to save.

"They'll try something else the next time," Whipple called. "We could move, but there must be a hundred of them out there. We've got no place to go and no horses now. Hang tight and hope Major Templeton will come to relieve us."

A minute later another rush came. This time they rode in fast, then stopped when they saw the Blue Shirts. It was a cat and mouse game. The Blue Shirts hid behind their trees. The Sioux moved on their horses. A pistol fired. Almost at once the trooper who shot was pierced by eight arrows.

Captain Whipple lay at the base of a big pine tree. He heard movement several yards away. The Sioux were sitting still on their mounts, waiting for the troopers to give themselves away. A soldier screamed something, then fired. A moment later a wail of terror came. Captain Whipple tried not to listen as the trooper begged them to stop.

Four Sioux stood around him. His face was a mass of blood. One held the point of his knife an inch from the trooper's eye, laughed, and jabbed the blade a half-inch into the trooper's eyeball. The man fainted. They ripped off his boots and pants, cut off his genitals, and pushed them into his mouth. The poor man returned to consciousness, gagging on his own flesh. He fainted again, and the Sioux tired of the sport. One warrior took his war hatchet and chopped off the trooper's head with one blow.

Captain Whipple dropped to his knees and began working his way through the brush and snow on his belly. He saw pony hooves ahead of him. Behind him he heard another of his men screaming from torture. Captain Whipple looked at his Colt cylinder.

Four shots left. Three rounds for the Sioux and one for him. He inched toward the pony hooves directly ahead of him and surged upward out of the brush. He fired three times, killing two savages and knocking a third off his horse. From the corner of his eye, he saw another warrior drawing his bowstring back. Whipple put the revolver to his head. Before the Sioux could let the arrow fly, the officer blew his brains out across the snow.

On the palisade of Fort Keogh, Cavanaugh heard firing come from the north—first a dozen shots, then hundreds in a prolonged barrage that indicated heavy fighting.

"Major Templeton is in deep trouble," he said to Lieutenant Powell. "We must assume now that he disobeyed orders and pursued the hostiles over the ridge. Just why we'll have to find out later. There must be a lot more Sioux out there than we figured."

The colonel narrowed his eyes and looked toward the sound of the gunfire. "Powell, our cavalry is all gone. I want you to take out the rest of the infantry. Round up ninety men and be ready to march in ten minutes. Take the last three ambulances with you and the remaining six horses to pull them. I want you to quick-time out, find Templeton, and return with him to the post. If that's not possible, determine what happened out there and bring back what's left of Templeton's command. Go now, Powell!"

The rest of the infantry units were whistled out of barracks and duty stations, and marched out the gate ten minutes later. Even at quick-step it would take them an hour to get anywhere near where the fighting was taking place. Colonel Cavanaugh watched the troops go with a hollow spot in his belly. He turned to his fort and realized it was almost bare of fighting men. If a force of Sioux came out of the woods to the south and overran the rear wall, Fort Keogh would be quickly lost. He went to his office and began sending his runners out with orders.

All men were released from the guard house and ordered to equip themselves for fighting and report to the parade ground. The quartermaster workers, civil and military, were armed and sent to the parade grounds as well. All civilians on post were advised of the seriousness of the situation. Those with no personal rifles were armed. The combined force on hand equalled 119 men. Men were posted along the walls of the fort, with one man at each loop hole facing north. Colonel Cavanaugh returned to the lookout to watch and wait.

Three hours after Lieutenant Powell had taken out the second rescue column, the lookouts spotted a rider tearing down the trail along Big Piney Creek near the Lone Pine Ridge. Colonel Cavanaugh met the rider at the gate.

"Colonel. I've a message to relay from Lieutenant Powell in the field. He's on the ridge and the valley below is filled with Indians, perhaps a thousand of them. He can find no evidence of Major Templeton's forces. He's returning to the fort."

An hour later, one of the lookouts called, "Wagons and men near the Big Sandy moving this way!" Colonel Cavanaugh checked with his glasses. Powell was at the head of the column. It took them another thirty minutes to cover the distance to the fort.

Colonel Cavanaugh waited at the gate. Lieutenant Powell left his party a quarter of a mile from the fort and galloped forward. His uniform was smeared with blood, as were his hands and face. He shrugged off aid and saluted his commanding officer.

"Colonel, in the wagons I have the remains of forty-nine of Major Templeton's men. They appear to have been slaughtered by overwhelming odds." Colonel Cavanaugh hurried Powell into his office, poured him a glass of whiskey, and received his report.

"We stayed on the ridge. The savages in the valley below jeered us, called insults and shouts, but they would not come to us and we were not going to go down into the murder canyon to meet them. I determined there were at least fifteen hundred and perhaps two thousand hostiles in the area.

"After an hour, the warriors slowly withdrew to the Potlatch Creek and moved across it, vanishing into the woods. After waiting a sufficient time, we marched down the trail toward the upper Potlatch Creek valley. On the end of the ridge, the part toward the fort, we found signs of a terrible battle."

Powell discovered the forty-nine slaughtered cavalry men behind rocks and other insufficient cover. From the signs, the men had fought until their ammunition was gone. Then they had been killed, stripped, mutilated, and shot full of arrows.

"A few were killed by bullets. Most died of arrows or knives. Many were terribly tortured. We found Major Templeton among them. From the powder burns on his head it's evident that he died by a self-inflicted gunshot wound rather than let himself be captured and tortured by the Sioux. We made no more contact with the hostiles. It's my guess that they have retreated with their booty. We found no horses and no weapons of any sort left on the field. There is no indication what happened to the rest of Templeton's command, some thirty-two cavalry troopers." Looking grim, Colonel Cavanaugh slapped Powell on the shoulder.

"A grim task, but well done, Lieutenant. Get yourself a bath and some sleep. We'll all be in our uniforms tonight. The Sioux may now attack the fort knowing that we're short on manpower after their big victory."

"Yes, sir. My men performed well, sir. I'm . . . I'm sorry about Templeton. He never should have gone over the ridge."

"True, even if he didn't know there were two thousand Sioux waiting for him. Get a bath and some sleep, Powell. We may need you later on tonight." Colonel Cavanaugh watched him walk away: The man was so tired he could hardly get one foot in front of the next. Then the colonel thought about the scout Kahnachee. The Indian had been right.

13

MORE THAN A HUNDRED RIFLES! THE SPIRITS HAD favored White Eagle and the Sioux warriors. It would be a day which would go down in the legends of the Sioux nation.

White Eagle rode from the battlefield, leaving his warriors to claim their booty of knives and other wonders from the bodies of the dead. These men, too, would be mutilated grievously in death so their spirits would be wounded in any afterworld conflict with the Sioux.

White Eagle rode to the place where the White Eyes' trail crossed Potlatch Creek. He was to meet here with the braves who had driven the horses around the ridge. Only part of them were there with the horses. He could hear rifle fire and cries of a battle not far off.

One of the Brule rode up to him and reported.

"They followed us, so we brought the horses and

rifles here, and others waited for the pony soldiers with a surprise near the small creek."

A few minutes later the battle sounds ceased and the warriors came straggling in, some with rifles or more captured horses, and the silly White Eyes' solider hats with the wide brims that kept the wearer from seeing Brother Sky. The war ponies of the dead also came back. Over each one's back lay a dead Sioux. There had been a few killed in each of the three battles. When all the war ponies had been led back and their burdens lay in the grass, White Eagle counted.

There were twenty-seven slain, at least one warrior from every branch of the Sioux and from every band. It was a high price to pay even for such a great victory. Fifteen warriors had been wounded. Some had serious hurts, others minor. Their wounds were bound up. All were able to ride.

White Eagle beckoned to Little Neck, who had been at the war camp for two weeks preparing for this attack.

"What will the White Eye general do now, Little Neck?" he demanded.

The Brule thought for a moment, then nodded. "White Eyes' pony soldier chief will send another group of soldiers to find out about the first ones. They will have many guns."

"Where will they come first?"

"To the Ridge of Many Snows. They will hear many guns here and come to the ridge and look down within two hours."

"Then we will keep many warriors in the battlefield, and wait for another band of White Eye soldiers to blunder into our trap."

The warriors moved the dead White Eyes so they could not be seen from the top of the ridge. Then they waited.

It was well into the afternoon before their scouts reported more White Eye soldiers. Only a few were on horses, but they had three wagons with them.

White Eagle watched from his position halfway up the slope. The leader of the soldiers looked down the trail. White Eagle rode into view, hooted, and called him a coward in the Sioux language. Then many of the warriors revealed themselves, and taunted them, but the soldiers would not come down into the jaws of the deadly Sioux ambush.

When it was plain the trap could not be sprung, White Eagle and his men started to withdraw from the canyon. White Eagle had one more talk with Little Neck. Then he gave the word and two thousand warriors moved out with their booty and their dead and wounded, heading back to the war camp. The battle was over.

That night there would be a grand victory dance. The dead would be honored. The next day they would leave for the Powder River and their winter camp. They could brag of their great achievements and their bravery under fire by many guns.

As night fell around Fort Keogh, Colonel Cavanaugh had every able-bodied man on alert at the walls ready to repel any attack. He talked with the scout, Kahnachee.

"Sioux warriors pleased with their victory. They capture many rifles and horses. Warriors will brag at council fire about their great victory."

"But what about the fort?" Colonel Cavanaugh asked. "Surely they must know that they dealt us a grievous blow. They must know that since they have killed so many of my men the defenses of the fort are severely weakened."

Kahnachee smiled. "Sioux think only of the present. Right now every warrior who captured rifle or horse, every one who counted coup or killed an enemy— every warrior is eager to get home to scream out his bravery and story of his valor."

"Then you think there's a good chance that the Sioux leaders won't follow up their victory with an attack on the fort?"

"Yes, no attack possible."

Colonel Cavanaugh kept his men on the Firing slots. His 119 duty-ready men, both military and civilian, were greatly enhanced by the return of Lieutenant Powell and the ninety men who had been on the relief mission.

"I still feel naked sitting here with so few soldiers," Cavanaugh confessed to Powell and Sergeant Major Flynn.

"Let's hope it's as the Arapaho indicated," Lieutenant Powell said. "Then the Sioux will storm back to their winter camp and grand council to brag about their victories." The young officer sighed. "That Sioux chief out there should have cut me off, and engaged me. He should have taken the rest of his fighting men and swarmed all over this fort. He could have taken it with not an unreasonable amount of casualties. Our best artillery men were killed out there. They could have overrun us by sheer numbers alone. By now we should be dead, the women and children should be slaves, and this fort burned right down to the ground."

"But we're not and we won't be," Colonel Cavanaugh said. "Not now. They've lost the advantage of splitting our force. Nevertheless, every man in the fort will stay ready to fight all night. We'll sleep in our clothes and our boots. Issue ammunition so every rifleman has a hundred and sixty rounds on his person at all times. The women and children will stay in the powder magazine tonight. One officer will be inside and it shall be locked up tight. That officer has my instructions not to allow any of the women to be taken prisoner in case we are overrun."

Cavanaugh reached in his desk drawer and took out the captain bars that he had once worn. He looked at Lieutenant Powell.

"I'm hereby promoting you by field necessity to the rank of captain. Your parents are already on their way to Washington. I've lost my two subordinates. You'll act as deputy fort commander. You're now brevetted a captain. How are the troops holding up?" Powell's eyes flushed with pleasure. "Stunned, worried, mourning the loss of so many men," he stammered. "But they haven't given up. There's a lot of fight in us yet."

Kahnachee sat to one side, listening. Colonel Cavanaugh turned to him. "Are you good at moving at night."

The scout nodded.

"Captain Powell will outfit you with a horse, with or without a saddle, as you prefer. I want you to go out now and see where the Sioux are."

"The Sioux have war camp close, maybe five miles. If they go below, they go to war camp. Maybe tomorrow morning they head down Powder River." Cavanaugh stared at the scout. "Fine. If they are at the war camp, stop there and see if they will leave in the morning."

The Arapaho raised his eyebrows. "Hired?"

Cavanaugh smiled and nodded. "Yes, for a month, a dollar a day."

"Good. I go."

Colonel Cavanaugh had Sergeant Major Flynn find Captain Johnson and bring him to the office. The thin, blond officer stood rigidly in front of the colonel's desk, his face set in a grim stare.

"Captain Johnson, you're in charge of the defense of the fort. The Sioux may withdraw to crow about their victories. On the other hand, they could well attack the fort. We'll know by tomorrow. Consolidate the companies in the barracks, moving half units in together, and grouping the stragglers. That way we'll cut down how much wood we burn to keep warm."

"Yes, sir. Double guards for tonight's stands?"
"Absolutely."

Cavanaugh looked at the wind-up clock on his desk. It was just past nine o'clock. "I want a meeting of all of the officers in the fort except the guard officer in fifteen minutes in my office. Round them up. Sergeant Major Flynn and the runners can help." "Yes, sir!" The captain saluted and hurried out. The fort's seven remaining officers, including Doctor Hines, were all there by the designated time. Three had died that day, including Lieutenant Ihander, who had gone with the wood detail.

"Gentlemen, we're in a critical situation. We're not sure where the Sioux warriors are. We think they come from a winter gathering on the Powder River about fifty miles north of us. An Arapaho scout is tracking them to determine where they are and what their intentions are. That leaves tonight as an issue. Captain Johnson is in charge of the guard. All troops will sleep in full fighting uniform, ready to go in a second. Any questions?"

"Sir, we've had no word from Captain Whipple. Are we to assume the worst?" Lieutenant Brown asked.

"I'm afraid so. He was with Major Templeton. Evidently he was separated from the major, or perhaps sent around to flank the position. In either case, with two thousand warriors down there, it would be a miracle if Whipple could have ridden out of danger."

There were no more questions. The strain showed clearly on his officers' faces.

"The next twelve hours are going to be rugged. Get some sleep if possible because at sunup we'll stay on full alert with every man available at the wall-firing loops and on the Howitzers." Colonel Cavanaugh looked around. "You're excused."

The men stood up and drifted outside.

Lieutenant Nate Brown motioned to Matt Colgan and they went out into the cold night air, walking well away from the other officers.

"Looks like our little surprise birthday party for Linda and Colonel Cavanaugh is called off," Brown said.

Matt Colgan groaned. "Damn, I'd forgotten all about that. Hell, there's no need to take the risk now that the major is dead. Christ, what a way to go. At least he did it quick with his own gun and wasn't tortured."

"Did you see some of those poor bastards?"

"See them? My men had to take the bodies out of the wagons and identify them. It's going to have to be a mass grave tomorrow if we can dig into the ground. It can't be frozen down more than a foot yet."

Brown shook his head. "Our party for the colonel seems stupid and ridiculous now, doesn't it? Linda said she'd be willing to go ahead. She thought Cavanaugh had ordered Major Templeton to take the rescue force out. I explained it to her."

"You suppose he'd still be alive if he hadn't gone down that damn trail the other side of the ridge?" Brown spat into the snow. "Hell, yes. It was a bloody trap all along. With two thousand hostiles out there just screaming for white blood, there wasn't a way in hell that any of those men could have survived. What puzzles me is why the Sioux didn't swarm all over Powell and his men when they went out in the afternoon. They could have sent a couple hundred around the ridge and cut off his retreat, then cut his men to pieces."

"The Sioux must have been satisfied with what they had."

"No doubt. We'll probably go out and bring the other bodies back tomorrow. They'll be frozen- like cord wood by then. That's going to be a horror story all its own."

"Damn, what a mess! But it looks like Cavanaugh is handling it the best anyone could."

Brown nodded. "Hate to admit it, but you're right. Wonder what Linda is going to say when I tell her I have to go to bed with my uniform and boots on." Colgan snorted. "You'll be sleeping on the couch or on the floor."

Lieutenant Brown picked the couch in the small living room.

14

THE SIOUX WARRIORS RETURNED TO THEIR WAR CAMP ON the banks of the upper Powder River. They stopped, even though they were only eight or nine miles from the pony soldiers' fort at Pine Woods. White Eagle kept a rear guard of forty warriors, but there were no White Eyes chasing them.

White Eagle took his place at the warming fire in the big lean-to, and counselled with the other chiefs. The night was for celebrating. At dawn, they would begin the two-day ride back to their tipis.

The flames of a giant bonfire roared into the sky. Gathered around it, the warriors told of their exploits. The stories went on and on. Long before everyone had spoken, White Eagle left the big fire and walked far enough away so the boasting voices could barely be heard. He lay down in the snow for a prayer vigil with the Great Spirit.

He gave thanks for his own safety and for the

success of the Sioux warriors. White Eagle vowed that he would walk in the moccasins of the great chiefs for all the days and the nights of his life. After a halfhour of praise and joy, White Eagle returned to the shelter, lay down in his soft buffalo calf robe, and quickly went to sleep.

In the morning, the Sioux prepared to leave. The captured horses and mules had been held in a rawhide corral. Each warrior had put a mark on his captured beast, and rawhide halters had been made for the animals. There was no order of march. Each band traveled together.

Fifty miles would be an easy one-day ride in the summer over the open prairie, but the deep snow and ice slowed their pace. Still, the trip went quicker than on the way down and at the end of the first day they had traveled more than thirty miles. The second day White Eagle's band pulled into their tribe's camp just before mid-afternoon. There was much shouting and joy at their arrival, and then much wailing and crying as the women of the tribe learned of the death of three warriors.

The wives of the three men, five in number, slashed their arms and their breasts. They wailed a loud lament until the sun went down, then dried their eyes, bound up their slashed bodies, and hurried to the council fire where the whole band had gathered to hear of the exploits of their warriors.

First White Eagle gave the gathered throng of warriors, women, and children a report on the raid. He told them how they surprised the woodlot crew and defeated the army sent to save them. They had killed every man and taken from them more than forty horses and more than 110 rifles and twenty-five pistols.

"Warriors in our own band captured twelve rifles and three pistols, and we will learn how to fire the weapons and where to find bullets to use against the White Eye soldiers."

Then he stepped back to a chorus of shouts and screeches of approval.

He lifted his right hand, and a warrior on his war pony charged toward the council fire. He skidded to a stop just short of the council. A buffalo hide had been pegged to the ground, and the warrior threw his lance into the robe. The point buried itself deep into the ground.

The warrior leaped to his horse's back, stood on it, and told how he had killed three White Eyes in the wood party. He described in glowing and graphic detail how he had courageously fought against great odds and overcome them, even though each had a rifle and one had an axe. He held up three scalps to prove his story. Two of them were black, but the third was bright red.

When his story was over, the warrior dropped onto the back of his horse and rode from the circle. At once another warrior raced in on horseback, drove his lance into the buffalo skin, and told his story.

It was a long, long ceremony. Sixty-five of the

warriors had tales to tell. White Eagle smiled as he listened to the feats of bravery under fire by the dreaded White Eye pony soldiers. Time after time, another warrior rode in and threw his lance into the buffalo hide. Soon there were thirty lances in it, then fifty covered the hide.

Drummers beat their drums and pounded them each time a warrior rode in or out. At last the final warrior rode out; tales of glory were over for the night. White Eagle came to his feet and faced the members of his band across the council fire.

"We are Sioux. We are Ogalala Sioux. This raid has shown us who are our friends and our blood. The People are strong. This show of force to the White Eye soldiers will drive them to leave their forts here and at Big Horn to the north. The pony soldiers will soon ride back toward the rising sun and the big Muddy River. When the White Eye soldiers leave, we will bum down the structures and return the valley to peace. This will bring the buffalo back and there will be good hunting once more. The People will grow in strength and number. We will prosper."

He signaled the drummers, who at once began the beat of the victory dance. A dozen warriors leaped to their feet and began to leap around the council fire. Others joined in until there were fifty warriors writhing and twisting in the flickering light of the orange flames.

White Eagle rose from his position in the council and walked to his lodge. Almost always, returning after days away, it was Many Skies who satisfied him. He lifted the flap of his tipi and found a hot rabbit stew and berry-flavored pemmican waiting for him. He warmed himself and ate. Then, smiling shyly, Many Skies came to him and they made love.

The next morning, White Eagle visited the tipis of the three slain men. In the first he found a family gathering. When a Sioux warrior married, he moved to the family duster of his wife to become a part of her family. His second wife and each new one after that also moved to his tipi and became a part of his first wife's family.

Now the tipi was without a hunter. Two wives and three children sat to one side and the first wife's father, Slow Foot, paced the tipi near the fire. He looked up when White Eagle arrived.

The slain warrior had no brother who could take in the family. White Eagle reminded Slow Foot that a warrior in their band was without a wife. His wife had died two weeks ago of some strange fever, leaving two small children.

"That is so, Chief White Eagle," Slow Foot said.

"Would Slow Foot be willing to accept a new husband into his family, one with two children and no wife?"

Slow Foot pondered the matter. He stared at the fire, then lit his pipe and drew three puffs. All this time the two widows cringed and wept. Slow Foot looked up once, scowled at them, and called for food. He and White Eagle ate a squirrel stew that had been readied.

When they had finished, Slow Foot took two more puffs from his pipe. Then he passed it to White Eagle.

Slow Foot nodded. "Yes, I have heard of this young man, Otter Paw. It is said he is a good hunter and that he counted coup on the raid with you. Yes, we will have him as son-in-law."

The next tipi with the grieving widows was an easier matter. The two widows had four children between them, three girls and a boy, but the dead man had four brothers. One of them had already accepted the wives and family. The young man had not married yet and was only nineteen. The family made the announcement and smoked the pipe with White Eagle. He went on to the next tipi.

The tipi was cold and there was no one in it. White Eagle went to the widow's father, Buffalo Horn. The warrior was older and a good friend of White Eagle.

They sat and smoked and at last the subject of his daughter came up. She was eighteen, and had been married only three months.

The squaw had returned to her father's lodge. Her tipi would be traded to the next newly-married couple for two horses. The young widow had no children. She would have no trouble finding a new husband. White Eagle was pleased with the arrangement.

Back at his tipi he lay on his buffalo robe and watched the fire. Someone brought him news of a petty dispute. No one knew how it began, but one of the smaller Sans Arcs bands would be moving away from the lower end of the gathering. They were going several miles farther down the Powder to a valley with dense timber and much firewood, where they could wait out the winter alone.

White Eagle smoked his pipe and considered it. There was no way anyone could talk them out of the move. Each band was free to come and go as the members wished. In fact, a warrior could move from one band to another. White Eagle called over his second wife and stroked her swollen belly. It would be soon now, a month, a winter baby. This one would be a boy. He patted her belly and sent her back to her work on new leggings for him.

The great war chief of all the Sioux settled down beside the fire. The desire of the warriors for blood and action was satisfied. For now they would live out the winter safe in their camp. Banded together this way, only a foolish White Eye general would order the pony soldiers to attack the Sioux.

Kahnachee lay in the snow a hundred yards from the last camp of the Sans Arcs on the Powder River. It was morning of the second day after the return of the warriors to their winter camp. The singing and feasting, dancing and bragging were over.

The night before, he had walked downstream five miles and seen many tipis. But he returned to the Sans Arcs because he heard an argument going on there. It was not between two warriors, but between two bands of Sans Arcs. It was an important argument. It was about a warrior's honor.

He was just about to move off and return to Fort

Keogh with his report when a sudden burst of activity made Kahnachee freeze. The band was moving!

Tipi poles dropped. The great spread of the tipi covering was pulled off and folded. The second band of Sans Arcs was preparing to move away from the huge encampment.

Kahnachee lay in the snow now without moving. The general activity in the area was reaching the frantic stage. Tipi poles were tied into a travois and steadied with cross braces. All the possessions of the family were packed in parfletches and bundled into buffalo robes, then wrapped and tied to the tipi poles. The travois would be pulled by a horse.

Two hours later, the chief, with his number one wife riding on the travois, led out to the south.

Kahnachee trailed the little band as they moved down the Powder River ten miles to a partially hidden valley heavily forested with thick brush. He watched them tramp down the snow, erect tipi poles, and tie them. Then the massive buffalo hides were unfolded and spread over the framework.

The Arapaho scout spent most of the day watching them. Then he moved down the Powder River, beginning the long journey back to Fort Keogh. Moving at night across the glowing snows, he encountered no one. He covered the distance just before dusk the next evening. Cold and exhausted, he presented himself to Colonel Cavanaugh and made his report.

15

Lieutenant Colonel Marcus Cavanaugh stayed up all night walking the wall. The guards knew he was coming around and that helped them stay alert. They had one scare when a big buck deer charged out of the brush almost at daylight, but they saw a cougar chasing it, and not surreptitious movement by Indian braves. The buck bounced away with ten-foot leaps, and the cougar retreated to the woods.

Cavanaugh leaned against the thick pine logs of the palisades, scarcely able to believe that they had not been attacked. It was a tactical blunder of the first order by the Sioux. He fought back his fatigue and decided to tend to business. His duty included talking to the widows of Major Templeton and Captain Whipple.

Nothing would be said to them about their husbands disobeying orders. Whatever the officers had done, they were dead now, and they would be allowed to rest in peace. He walked slowly back to his office. Sergeant Major Flynn had kept a fire going there all night, and was dozing quietly in a corner of the room. The colonel let him sleep.

Cavanaugh's first order of business was to check the wood supply. With the men reorganized into fewer companies, the barracks' needs were cut to a minimum to maximize the use of wood. He also had to get a dispatch out by courier to inform headquarters of the losses. He would spell it out in detail, noting the standing order not to go down that trail. He would also send along an urgent request for three hundred infantry and a hundred cavalry fully equipped to be marched to his post at once. Then scouts had to check on the location of the bodies they had to recover and watch for any sign of Sioux.

He left his office without waking Sergeant Major Flynn, and went across the parade ground to the powder magazine. The two men on guard outside saluted him sleepily.

"Let them out!" he ordered. "We're safe enough for the time being." The double doors of the powder magazine were unbolted and pulled open. The women and children struggled out with sleeping bundles, sleepy-eyed and cold. Cavanaugh greeted them, assured them all was well, and then when they were on their way to their quarters, he hurried to his own. Lloyd had the fire going and breakfast ready. Cavanaugh ate, drank a big cup of coffee, and then returned to his office.

Sergeant Major Flynn sat at his desk, wide awake. His coffee cup was half-full.

"Sir, we're still here this morning."

"And we have lots of work to get done."

He ordered Lieutenant Colgan to take a party of six on the scouting expedition. They were unmounted. If all was well, a runner was to return as soon as possible, and wagons would be sent out for the dead. Then Cavanaugh sent for the stable sergeant, a tobacco-chewing, former cowboy who knew horses better than anyone else on the post. He was nearly forty years old, but had been in the army only ten years. He slouched into the colonel's office and gave a terrible salute, which Cavanaugh waved aside.

"Peterborough, how many horses and mules do we have fit for work?"

"Six mules, sir, and seven, maybe eight horses, including your mount."

"I want you to get together mule teams for four wagons. We've got the bodies of sixty-six of our men out there somewhere. Have the wagons ready to roll in a half hour and stand by."

"Yes, sir," Sergeant Peterborough said. He hurried out the door.

Colonel Cavanaugh drained his coffee and poured himself a fresh cup from the pot on the stove in the outer office. A new pot had been made, and it was almost full. It was just after six o'clock, too early to call on the widow Templeton.

He had a runner bring Captain Powell and asked for

a report on the reorganization of the barracks. One company was gone entirely. Half of two other units were dead. There were bits and pieces of another company and the whole cavalry unit had been slaughtered.

Captain Powell stood before the commander's office without the strength to salute. Cavanaugh took a long look at him.

"Powell, one of us has to be awake around here.

You're to report to your quarters and sleep until you're awakened. That will probably be about noon when I'm going to be falling down or sleeping standing up. When you get back here this afternoon, I want you to write a report of your rescue mission yesterday. Write it exactly as it happened."

"Yes, sir. But I was working with the barracks reorganization."

"Who else is there?"

"Captain Johnson and Lieutenant Brown."

"They can handle it. Get out of here and get some sleep."

When Powell had gone, Cavanaugh looked at his list. He added Kahnachee on the end. Where was that savage? He would have found the Sioux by now and reported back, unless the Sioux had left the area. In that cast, Kahnachee would follow them. He could be gone four or five days.

Cavanaugh was itching to make a strike against the Sioux who hit them, and in order to stop them from attacking again, he would have to. With his limited resources, however, it was impossible to attack two thousand warriors in one huge winter gathering. Until Kahnachee returned, however, he could not develop strategy.

Again he looked over his list and sent for the woodlot sergeant. He reported in quickly.

"Yes, sir. My best estimate with two fewer barracks being heated is that we now have a forty-one days' supply of wood." The sergeant was thanked, and he left the office.

At nine o'clock, Colonel Cavanaugh went to see the widow Templeton. Her children were in Omaha with a relative. It was going to be the hardest call of all.

Viola Templeton answered his knock on the door of her quarters. She knew why he was there. She had dressed and the fire was going. She smiled at Cavanaugh and asked him to sit. She automatically began to knit.

"Colonel, I know why you're here, and you don't have to say the usual things. I know you and Sawyer had some problems. He was so proud of this fort. When you said it was the finest stockaded fort in the nation he was terribly pleased. Now, I'll want to be going back to Omaha where our children are staying with my sister. I've been ready for this day most of my life in the army. I had a major's wife lecture me when I was new to the army and at our first post. She said every day with an army officer is to be treasured. She told me she had lost one officer husband. It could come at any time and an army wife had to be ready for it. She told me always to plan that my husband would be killed. If he wasn't, I would be thankful. If he was, I would be ready. Colonel, I'm ready."

She put down her knitting finally, and despite the control she had over her emotions, tears welled in her eyes. "Now, I know there won't be any transport available for the sixty-mile-run to Fort Reno for a time. I'd guess if we get more of this warming spell an ambulance could get through in a week or so. We'll watch the weather."

Mrs. Templeton signaled, and the orderly brought in a tray with coffee.

"Never seen an army man who couldn't stand another cup of coffee." She sipped at the strong brew and looked up. "Colonel, how many men did we lose yesterday?"

"We're not sure about Captain Whipple, but it's almost for sure that he and his men are lost, as well. That would make it a hundred and seventeen."

Violet Templeton shook her head and dabbed at her eyes. "So many, so many." She recovered quickly. "Well, I know you have a lot to do this morning, Colonel. Did you have anything else to tell me?"

"No, Mrs. Templeton. My condolences. We'll arrange a separate grave for your husband, of course."

"Thank you."

She stood. Colonel Cavanaugh thanked her again and left by the front door.

Back at the office, he sent for Captain Johnson. When he came, they talked for a few minutes about the chances of an attack on the fort. Then the colonel got to his point.

"Captain, I want you in charge of the graves. Check the ground. We'll continue to use the area out the south gate for our cemetery. Set up a detail to erect a rail fence around the plot. I would think that separate graves for the three officers is appropriate and a mass grave for the men. It's the only practical way we can handle it. Any suggestions?"

"No, sir. Shall I begin digging the graves at once?" "Yes."

Just after the captain left, the runner from the scouting patrol returned with the news that there was no sign of Sioux. They had found the remains of Captain Whipple and his cavalry on Potlatch Creek, a mile west of the crossing with the Westward Trail.

"Sir, Lieutenant Colgan said he would wait for the wagons there and I should direct them."

The private was sent to the stable area where the four wagons were dispatched.

Now that Cavanaugh was certain of the death of Captain Whipple, he called on the widow. She was stiff-faced, angry, and barely civil. He expressed his sorrow, and told her they would arrange transport for her and Mrs. Templeton as soon as possible.

Back in his office, Colonel Cavanaugh looked at the pad of paper and the pen and ink bottle on his desk and sighed. He had to write a report and send it off today with two dispatch riders. The next two or three days were going to be gruesome.

Two days later, the graves were dug and false graves were marked so Indian Marauders would not find the bodies. The service was read by Marcus to a solemn gathering.

Cavanaugh wrote a detailed report to General Cooke about the massacre. Two volunteers took the dispatch to Fort Reno. For a day, the fort settled down into a more normal routine. The place seemed half deserted. Colonel Cavanaugh and Captain Powell tried to maintain normal procedures and discipline.

Wood details went out toward the brush and pine immediately behind the fort and cleared a stretch along Little Sandy Creek. Some of the larger trees were cut for wood, as well as a dozen pines. The next day, Kahnachee returned. Colonel Cavanaugh made sure he had a good meal first, then brought him into his office.

"I would guess the Sioux have gone back to their winter quarters north of the Powder River."

"Yes, Colonel. But two bands leave main group. One north into Montana. One come south on Powder."

Colonel Cavanaugh leaned forward. "How big a band?"

"Sixty tipis. Sans Arcs Sioux. They have shod army horses in their brushy corral."

"How far from here," Cavanaugh said, his voice tight.

"Forty-five miles on Powder River."

"Kahnachee, can you lead us back there?"

"Yes."

"Get a good night's sleep and eat all you want. We'll be heading up the Powder River tomorrow."

Colonel Cavanaugh made his arrangements at once. He called out troopers who had been in the army more than a year. He had a group of sixty, all infantry.

He began rejecting men for various reasons. A few looked sickly and too small to make the march. At last he had what looked like a good troop. There were forty-five men and four sergeants.

He picked Lieutenant Matt Colgan to go with him, and told the men to check their equipment. They all had overcoats and would be issued 160 rounds of ammunition. They would leave at dawn the next day.

The fort buzzed with activity. Captain Powell stood in the commander's office watching him.

"This means a lot to you, doesn't it, Colonel? A chance to strike back at some of the Sioux that wounded us so terribly."

"Damn right, it means a lot. Also, I've got to have an attack against them on the books or General Cooke will fry me in a skillet."

"I'm not going along?"

"True. You're in charge of the fort until I return. Hell, you're in charge also if I don't return. I can't risk you on the attack."

"Why would one band of Sans Arcs Sioux pull away from the protection of the rest of the Sioux?" Powell asked.

"Kahnachee said there was a hell of a big argument about something, the honor of the warriors or something. He couldn't be sure because of the language difference. Anyway the two units pulled out. One went north, this one came south. He said it looks like a prime camp area."

The troops left at dawn the next day. There were fifty-two of them altogether, forty-five troopers, four sergeants, the two officers, and the scout, Kahnachee. Colonel Cavanaugh and Kahnachee led the march. They hiked through the snow to Big Sandy Creek, which ran into Clear Creek before the latter hit Powder River.

The men had hardtack and salt pork for six days in their packs. They marched along in a column of twos with their rifles on slings over their shoulders.

Kahnachee figured they could make twelve miles a day. He worked ahead half a mile as they went up on the far side of the creek. Soon they picked up the broad path made by the Sioux on their return to their camp.

"No scouts, no lookouts," Kahnachee had told Colonel Cavanaugh. "They think they are safe in winter camp."

They marched for twelve miles the first day and spent the night in some brush under simple shelters. The next morning they were on the trail again. They had a quick stop at noon to rest and eat, and then stopped for good at about five that afternoon.

They stopped again the next evening just before five o'clock.

"Winter camp Sans Arcs a mile away," Kahnachee said.

Colonel Cavanaugh said that would attack at dawn. He ordered the men to make a silent camp. There was to be no talking and no fires. He and the scout moved ahead to reconnoiter the target. They lay under a fringe of pine trees and looked down at the small camp.

"Sixty tipis must mean sixty warriors, right, Kahnachee?"

The Arapaho nodded. "No tipi long without warriors and hunters," he said.

Colonel Cavanaugh looked over the situation. The tipis took up almost the whole length of the small finger valley. There was no outlet at the top, only where the stream flowed into the Powder at the bottom. He reasoned out his strategy quickly. He would put twenty troopers on each side of the valley for a crossfire, then the other twelve would be downstream in a blocking position. They would let women and children through but kill any warriors who tried to come that way.

Satisfied, he pushed back from the ridge line and hiked to the encampment where his troops lay in their small lean-to shelters. Colonel Cavanaugh told the sergeants to group the men around him.

"Gentlemen, a mile from here, over that next ridge to the left, is a band of sixty tipis of a Sans Arcs Sioux camp. They have no scouts, and no lookouts. They think they are safe in their winter nest. Tomorrow morning at dawn they will learn differently. There are families in those tipis. No man shall deliberately fire into a tipi. We are here to kill their warriors, not their women and children."

He paused a moment to let his words sink in. Then he outlined his plan. "We will place a force on each side of the small valley, and a smaller group of men downstream toward the Powder. River in a blocking position. In this downstream direction, the women and children are to be allowed to pass. The warriors are to be shot on sight. We will not scatter their horse herd, since we believe there are army mounts there and others that could be trained to be army mounts. We'll take the whole herd back to the fort with us if possible. Now, are there any questions?"

"Will we be charging into the camp, sir?"

"Toward the last. We hope to clean it out from our fixed position. Then we'll move in and check it." There were no more questions and the men were sent back to their blankets to get what sleep they could.

Colonel Cavanaugh assigned the four sergeants to the three attack positions and one to help control the horses and war ponies in the small rawhide corral.

When dawn wakened the sleeping, snow-clad valley the next morning, the troops were in position. Colonel Cavanaugh had the near side, Lieutenant Colgan the far side, and Sergeant Burns was with the twelve men in the block.

As the daylight pierced the dark, eastern sky, Cavanaugh waited for the first stirring below. He wanted it light enough to be able to select targets. The sky brightened. He could pick out the different tipis.

His men looked at him. A warrior stepped out of his tipi and headed behind it to the edge of the brush to relieve himself. It was time.

Cavanaugh lifted his hand. When he dropped it, four rifles barked, and the warrior met the great spirit.

The rounds brought a flurry of activity below. A dozen warriors raced from their tipis, some grasping bows and arrows, some furiously trying to load the new rifles they had captured. The seasoned hands on both sides of the valley began picking off the warriors as they raced from their lodges.

For a moment all was quiet, then more warriors ran from the tipis with their women and children in a sudden burst of activity. Cavalry rifles barked again and again.

One warrior broke and raced toward the war ponies. Three rounds cut him down before he was halfway there. Half a dozen well-placed shots stopped a knot of warriors, making them dead men. Confusion quickly replaced the sniper fire. More than a hundred Indians raced around the tipis, with the women and children fleeing to the north along the stream.

Most of them passed the blocking force. Others followed. Some of the warriors tried to get to the brush behind the tipis only to find a steady stream of fire aimed at them.

Two warriors retreated inside their tipis, and quickly found out that they had a haven. No rounds pierced the hides. They cut small firing holes in the sides and sniped at the Blue Shirts, who were firing from the brush-covered hill.

Fifteen minutes after the firing began, the camp was silent. Two small children wandered around crying, almost naked in the snow. A dozen dead Sioux could be seen on the ground.

"Charge!" Captain Cavanaugh bellowed. His men rose up on both flanks and moved down the hill.

A flurry of firing came from one tipi. The three warriors who had holed up inside ran out, swinging war axes and firing with bows and arrows. One slashed at a trooper with his hatchet. The nearest trooper slammed the butt plate of his rifle into the Sans Arc's head, crushing it and dropping him into the snow. The other two warriors were shot as they surged from their cover. Suddenly, the snow-and- ice-clogged valley was deathly silent.

Cavanaugh took a casualty report.

Lieutenant Colgan smiled as he saluted and reported in. "Sir, we have three men with swollen ankles. We are arranging for them to ride as soon as we can fashion hackamores. One man was grazed by a Sioux bullet, but the bleeding on his arm has stopped. Another man had a minor slash from a war axe and our last casualty has a serious headache."

Both officers laughed to relieve the tension.

"We do have one dead trooper, sir. He's been tied over a horse on a lead line."

One woman had been killed in the melee, but no children were dead.

Now began the tough job of checking each tipi. They found only two old men and two babies. All four were taken out and let go. They shuffled downstream to freedom and safety. When the tipis had been cleared, Colonel Cavanaugh ordered the burning to begin.

"I want everything of value destroyed. All of the tipi coverings, the tipi poles, every bit of food, all those fancy rawhide boxes, all the buffalo robes, everything. I don't want a stick or a pot left the Sioux can use."

It took them three hours to finish burning and destroying the camp.

Colonel Cavanaugh went to look at the horses. The sergeant and Kahnachee had kept the animals in check during the shooting and killed two warriors who crept through the fire fight to get to the corral. Their bodies were freezing quickly in the snow.

There were eight or ten army mounts that he could quickly identify. Among the other mounts were a number that could be turned into cavalry animals, or at least wagon horses. There were over a hundred horses altogether.

"We'll take the whole herd with us," Cavanaugh told Kahnachee. "Grab yourself a war pony and pick out two or three of the old army mounts that you can make a quick hackamore for. We'll find some men who can ride to help you herd them home."

They left the smoldering village half an hour later. Lieutenant Colonel Marcus Cavanaugh settled down on the back of the army mount Kahnachee had provided for him. If he pushed his men, they would be back in Fort Keogh in two days. Kahnachee said the chances of any pursuit by the other Sioux were not great.

"They did not like when this band left gathering. Even other Sans Arcs would be slow to follow. We have good head start and Sans Arcs have many new women and children to care for. They will be busy for two days. Warriors are not ready to make another fight with White Eyes."

Colonel Cavanaugh didn't expect any pursuit. The Sioux would have a hard time topping their last victory. They would save their anger for another target. Colonel Cavanaugh rode along slowly, watching his troops marching home victorious. Small as it was, the counterattack would help rebuild spirit at the fort. There would be repercussions in Washington from the Templeton massacre, but he would get another report off to Omaha about his retaliatory raid against the Sioux. It would not hurt his cause. And he had confidence that General Sheridan would replace the lost men and increase the numbers at the fort. In spring there would be an all-out Indian war against the Sioux.

The cavalry was his life and he wouldn't choose any other profession, pure hell as it was sometimes. He kicked the mount in the flanks and rode up to check on the head of the column. They were heading home!

A LOOK AT LONG ROAD TO ABILENE

BY ROBERT VAUGHAN

LONG ROAD TO ABILENE, is a classic hero's journey, a western adventure that exemplifies the struggles, the defeats, and the victories that personify the history of the American West. After surviving the bloody battle of Franklin and the hell of a Yankee prison camp, Cade McCall comes home to the woman he loves only to find that she, believing him dead, has married his brother. With nothing left to keep him in Tennessee, Cade journeys to New Orleans where an encounter with a beautiful woman leads to being shanghaied for an unexpected adventure at sea. Returning to Texas, he signs on to drive a herd of cattle to Abilene, where he is drawn into a classic showdown of good versus evil, and a surprising reunion with an old enemy.

AVAILABLE NOW

ABOUT THE AUTHOR

Robert Vaughan sold his first book when he was 19. That was 57 years and nearly 500 books ago. He wrote the novelization for the miniseries *Andersonville*. Vaughan wrote, produced, and appeared in the History Channel documentary *Vietnam Homecoming*. His books have hit the NYT bestseller list seven times. He has won the Spur Award, the PORGIE Award (Best Paperback Original), the Western Fictioneers Lifetime Achievement Award, received the Readwest President's Award for Excellence in Western Fiction, is a member of the American Writers Hall of Fame and is a Pulitzer Prize nominee. Vaughn is also a retired army officer, helicopter pilot with three tours in Vietnam. And received the Distinguished Flying Cross, the Purple Heart, The Bronze Star with three oak leaf clusters, the Air Medal for valor with 35 oak leaf clusters, the Army Commendation Medal, the Meritorious Service Medal, and the Vietnamese Cross of Gallantry.